HOUSE OF SIX

EVIL LIES WITHIN

JACK HEATH

NARROW
ESCAPE
PRESS

NARROW ESCAPE PRESS

Narrow Escape Press, Midland Park, NJ

ISBN eBook: 978-1-959760-03-0

ISBN Paperback: 978-1-959760-04-7

ISBN Paperback (Large Print): 978-1-959760-05-4

For Patty...

PROLOGUE

The girl's feet kicked up small puffs of dust as she walked down the dirt lane. The greens, blues, and reds of her plaid skirt seemed to pulse with every step, and the wind tossed the blazer covering her white blouse, each gust making it rise and writhe as if trying to escape the strain of her backpack straps. Her hair was dark, tied in a neat ponytail, and her face had a youthful glow that betrayed her age. She was at best thirteen, fourteen.

The sky overhead was a swirl of heavy gray clouds that threatened rain, yet the path was hard and bone dry. An ancient stone wall ran along beside the lane; and beyond, the ground rose to what should have been a verdant meadow. Instead, sheep grazed on scabby brown grass that clung to the hillside.

The man looked down on the scene with growing dread. Something was terribly wrong. He called to the girl, imploring her to turn around, to go back to wherever she had come,

but his voice, barely escaping his mouth, faded into the heavy

gauze of the approaching storm. He tried to run after her, but his movements were slow and restrained, like a fly trapped in ether.

This was a dream, he *knew* it was a dream, but through the horror of his past he understood that something about this dream was more, was real. The man cried out, screaming at the top of his lungs, but the girl kept walking.

Up ahead of her an enormous oak webbed the ground with twisted shadows, its barren limbs catching what little light there was, and deeper, beyond the edge of the shadows, was pitch black, as if some terrible secret was hiding in the darkness, waiting for the girl there—something he could feel, something he knew with all his senses was horrible beyond words, that related to another place, another girl.

Suddenly, his dream changed, and he saw the place where he had found the other girl. It was a room of white tiles with shackles set into the walls, the girl's nude body sagging in the chains, her belly slit open and her intestines spilling obscenely, the floor pooled with blood. The young girl, the one with the backpack, was walking into the exact same fate.

John Andrews bolted awake, his body tense with panic, his heart pounding, his pillow, and sheets soaked with his sweat. Beside him Amy gripped his shoulder and switched on the bedside lamp.

"John," she said, her voice soft yet urgent. "It's okay. You were having a dream."

Andrews pulled up his knees and brought his head

forward, balling himself up like a child hiding from the world. "The Coven," he groaned.

"It's over," Amy assured him as she worked her fingers into his shoulders, trying to unknot the muscles. "They're all dead, all of them. They can't hurt anyone anymore."

John tried to focus on the warm light from the lamp, the reassuring touch of Amy's hands on his shoulders, on the words she was speaking. More than anything, he wanted to believe her and be assured the Coven had finally been destroyed.

He was safe in his bed on Pickering Wharf in Salem, Massachusetts, he told himself. He wasn't on a dusty lane in God-knows-where. There wasn't a girl in danger. Amy was right. The Coven was gone. Hadn't he seen the bodies of the leaders? There was no mistaking the fact that they were dead because he was the one who had killed them, all of them except his friend Rich Harvey, who had killed himself, and he had seen that with his own eyes, too.

It was hard to imagine that all those things had taken place just a week earlier. Already it seemed like another life- time or another world because the discoveries had been so horrifying, the violence so unbelievable.

John knew that over the past week his mind had shut down, and shocked into a state of suspended animation. He hadn't thought about the Coven; he hadn't relived the bloody scenes. He had just gone through his days with his mind almost blank, getting up, taking long walks, eating, sleeping, never allowing himself to process the

atrocities of the previous weeks.

Now he realized he was starting to come out of it and re-enter the real world, and he was enough a student of psychology to know that nightmares were a natural part of reawakening. This bad dream wouldn't be the last one, and it was perfectly normal.

Only something nagged at him. He remembered something Captain Card said when they were alone together in the underground warrens of the Coven. John hadn't thought about it until now, but he was sure that Card said there had been a seventh member of the Coven. Card, a Massachusetts State Police detective, had been very cryptic and tight-lipped, and the few things he had let slip seemed to have only leaked out by accident. John wracked his brain to recall what else Card had said. He recalled something about the fact that the ultimate leader of a Coven was called the Inquisitor, and hadn't Card also said that all the Covens were organized the same way?

All the Covens, plural? The word had sat in his brain for the past week like a cancer, silent and waiting to be discovered. John felt a sickness deep inside. His mind reeled and images and memories of visions past—visions of Rebecca Nurse—came flooding back. As hard as he had tried at first to deny those visions of his long-dead relative, he had finally accepted that they were real. Now the same part of him that knew Rebecca Nurse had been real knew what he had just seen was no dream. The girl was real, and she was still walking, just entering the deep shade beneath the

ancient tree. What waited for her there was the same evil he

had defeated before; he could feel it. That meant the Coven might be gone from Salem, but it wasn't destroyed.

John sat up and turned to face Amy. "What?" she asked, seeing the alarm etched on his face.

"It's not over. It's not even close to being over."

PART 1

CHAPTER ONE

When John Andrews walked downstairs the next morning to make coffee, he stopped at the bottom of the staircase and investigated the living room at the portrait of his ancestor, Rebecca Nurse.

"Please talk to me," he said, gazing up at the painting. Just like almost any portrait of a Puritan woman, Rebecca

Nurse was unquestionably not pretty in her black dress with a high white collar. She sat in a rocking chair working on a piece of embroidery as her unsmiling face gazed out of the portrait.

Until very recently, John had hated the portrait, which had come as part of the furnishings of the house he'd inherited from his great aunt. His aunt's one condition on giving him the house had been that Rebecca's portrait had to remain

hanging in the house. For years John had never understood his aunt's reasoning, but he had honored that condition, hanging the portrait out of sight.

He used to joke that Rebecca Nurse had been "as ugly as a Rottweiler with a sore ass," but that was before the spirit of Rebecca Nurse helped him avenge the murder of his late wife. Until a few weeks ago, John Andrews would have scoffed at the idea of spirits, and when Rebecca first appeared to him, he had feared he was losing his mind. However, after the events of the past few weeks, his cynicism, or what he might have called his reporter's skepticism, was gone. He no longer had any doubt spirits existed or that they could communicate with the living, or, for that matter, that Devil worshippers had been living around him in Salem.

The Coven had operated in Salem for the past three hundred years and been responsible not only for the Salem witch trials, of which Rebecca Nurse had been the final victim, but also for countless blood sacrifices over the intervening centuries. John Andrews knew he was a man whose sense of certainty about everything in life barely existed.

In fact, he now acknowledged that the spirit of Rebecca Nurse was the reason he had survived the events of the past month. She had been the key to unlocking the Coven's foul secrets and had shown him the secret door that allowed him to attack them in their underground lair. In so doing she had opened him up to the mystical or spiritual power—whatever it had been, he still had no idea what to call it—that had allowed him to kill the leaders of the Coven. As a result, John had moved Rebecca's portrait and it now hung where it belonged, in the place of highest respect and visibility in his home, right above the mantelshelf.

As a professional journalist, Andrews was trained to question everything, and find the facts to support a story. These days he not only believed that the spirits of the dead could communicate with the living, but he also missed having that communication and wished Rebecca Nurse would continue to guide him as she had in the days when they struggled together against the Salem Coven. However, as if their victory over the Coven had somehow released her spirit to go wherever spirits went when they were at peace, Rebecca Nurse remained silent as she had in the days following Andrews's ultimate battle with the Salem Coven.

Andrews stood in front of the painting for another few seconds. "Not talking to me again today? You even there anymore, or have you gone on permanent vacation? Not that you don't deserve a permanent vacation, of course, after every- thing that happened to you. I hope you're someplace with palm trees and a sunny beach and people to bring you those little drinks with umbrellas in them. And no offense, but I hope you can finally get out of those heavy black clothes, put on shorts and sandals." Finally, he shrugged, knowing anyone who overheard him would think he was absolutely nuts, and he went to the front door to bring in the morning papers. He grabbed *The New York Times, Wall Street Journal,* and *Washington Post,* tossed them onto the counter, went to the coffeemaker and hit the on button then went back, pulled the papers from their plastic tubes, and started scanning the morning headlines.

He always read *The New York Times* first and skimmed over the paper's descriptions of disasters and conflicts around the world: another battle in Afghanistan, a car bombing in Iraq targeting Shiites, flooding in Thailand, a riot over growing unemployment in Spain. Strangely, when Andrews read world events, he found they relaxed him. At least these were straightforward things that happened month in and month out, year after year. A man could deal with wars, famines, and floods, he joked to himself, but not with Satan-worshipping Covens doing blood sacrifices in his own backyard.

As the aroma of brewing coffee filled the kitchen Andrews started to feel better, and his memory of the nightmare that had awakened him a brief time earlier faded from his memory. That was when he turned the page and saw the article about a drought in Great Britain. Something about it nagged at him, and he saw the girl from his dream again, her foot- steps kicking up small puffs of dust. The dream's setting with the rural lane, the stone wall along the road, and the grassy hillside with herds of sheep had been so quintessentially British, all except for the dryness.

Preoccupied with matters closer to home and he didn't think he'd even been aware the U.K. was suffering a drought. Why would he have dreamed it? Was it just a coincidence? Did the dream mean something, or was it simply a bad dream? He couldn't shake the feeling it meant something, and the whole thing gave him chills.

He stepped over to where he had his cell phone on the charger to look up the number for Captain Andrew Card. Card was a Massachusetts State Police detective John had taken down into the warren of underground passages to show Card where he had fought and killed the leaders of the Coven. However, when they had reached the room where the fight took place, John was shocked to find that the dead bodies and all the other evidence was missing. As stupefied as John had been, Card had seemed unsurprised, and that was when he had let slip the fact that he knew far more about the Covens and Devil worship than he had previously admitted.

John had tried calling Card multiple times since they'd discovered the bodies were missing, but Card had never returned his calls. John assumed the detective was extremely busy, and that he'd also probably assumed John wanted to talk things out, rehash what had happened and ask a lot of questions Card might be unwilling to answer.

Still, those questions had been eating at him. How much more did Card know? Why wasn't he willing to be more forth- coming? John needed answers, not only because the journalist inside him craved information, but also because what he had said to Amy earlier in bed was true. It wasn't over. He felt it in his guts like an essential truth, but he couldn't say why. He needed someone who knew more than he did to help him understand, but there was no doubt in his mind the danger still existed. It wasn't as close as it had been, but it was out there in the darkness. His nightmare had been a reminder of that truth, but was it more? Was it an omen of something in the future or a warning he should act on now? He needed to know these things. As foolish as he might sound recounting all this to anyone else, he was willing to take the risk, and Card was the only person John could think of to call.

Card's cell phone rang until a recording asked John to leave a message.

"Andrew," John said, leaving another message. "I had a dream last night and... look, I know this sounds crazy, but I'm quite sure I saw a girl who was about to be abducted by the Coven. But it wasn't this, Coven; it was a different one, someplace else. In England, but I can't be certain. It looked like England, but it could have been anyplace. I don't know who else to tell this to. Please call me."

CHAPTER TWO

An hour later, after three cups of strong coffee, John shoved his concern about the nightmare into the background and forgot about the Coven enough to focus on what he liked to call "the real world," which for him was the *Salem News*, the daily paper where he was executive editor.

Five minutes to eight, he and Amy walked out the door and headed up Pickering Wharf towards the newspaper offices. Finally able to get out of his own head, John noticed Amy had been unusually quiet that morning. She had come downstairs right before they needed to leave, grabbed a quick cup of coffee, and chugged it. Their relationship was new, it has only been a few weeks since it had moved into something more than just a friendship, John wasn't sure how to interpret her silence or what, if anything, to say or do.

Now as they walked along Salem's streets of sixteenth- and seventeenth-century houses, Amy held her arms tight across her chest, perhaps because of the early morning chill and damp wind that gusted off the Atlantic, but perhaps because she was upset.

"Something the matter?" John asked after they had gone a block in silence.

"What did you mean when you said it's not over?" she asked.

He took a deep breath, wondering how much he should tell her. It wasn't that he wanted to keep anything from her, quite the opposite in fact, but he knew how much of a terrible shock she had been through, nearly losing her life to the Coven in a blood sacrifice. He was reluctant to burden her with more. He glanced at her hands, still bandaged from where Cabby Corwin had cut them in the first stages of the sacrifice.

She caught him looking and said in a sharper tone, "What did you mean, John?"

He shook his head and blew out the breath he'd been holding. "I saw something in my dream last night, a girl walking along a country lane. It wasn't local; it was another part of the world, but she was walking into terrible danger."

"It was a nightmare."

"Yes," he said in a halting voice.

"But you think it was real somehow, don't you?"

He ran a hand over his face. "I can't help but think... I just don't know."

"John," she said, laying a hand on his arm, "you've been through unbelievable stress. We both have."

"I know," he said, wanting to believe that she was right, and stress was the cause, "but I keep thinking about my last conversation with Andrew Card."

Amy nodded. "And he told you there are Covens other places."

"Yes."

"But they're not here. That counts for something."

John shook his head. "That's not true. I killed the leaders of the Coven, but I'm sure that wasn't all of them. We have no idea how many are out there. Rich Harvey, my *friend*, was one of them. I look around this city and every person I see, I wonder if they're a member of the Coven. I wonder who I can trust, who I'll ever be able to trust."

"You sound paranoid."

"That's because I *am* paranoid. Aren't you?"

She was quiet for half a block before she said, "Yes, I'm feeling very paranoid, too, but it really makes me angry. I don't want to worry that every person in this town might be a secret Devil worshipper. I don't want to think that this is just *our* problem."

"You're suggesting that we're supposed to ignore them?"

She shook her head and looked at the ground. "No, of course not. I just feel like these people have invaded our lives, and I want them gone. I want the world to be what I always thought it was before a week ago, a place where there were a few bad people, but mostly good people and the Devil didn't really exist."

"But the world wasn't *really* that way at all. We just thought it was. Do you really want to be ignorant?"

She let out a humorless laugh and put her arm through his and gave it a squeeze. "No, but I also don't want to be looking over my shoulder for the rest of my life, wondering if the person behind me on the sidewalk or in the supermarket line is really a Devil worshipper who wants to kidnap me and kill me in a blood sacrifice."

"So, how do we keep from letting that happen?"

Amy shook her head, but then she got a fresh burst of spirit. "Tell me about your dream. Where did you think this girl was? Vermont?"

John shook his head. "It could have been, but I'm pretty sure it was England."

"Why England?"

"I don't know, maybe the stone walls or the hills and the sheep, maybe the gray sky."

"Where in England?" "Haven't got a clue."

He felt a shudder go through her, and she asked, "What do you think you're supposed to do about dreams like that?"

"I don't know."

The walked another half block in silence, but then Amy let out a reluctant sigh. "You're right. If you have dreams like that and you think they're real, you can't just do nothing."

John nodded, finally putting words to what had been bothering him since he woke up. "I know. If I try to ignore them, they'll drive me insane, but how do I do something to save a girl who's walking on a road, and I don't know where in the world it is?"

She squeezed his arm, but she could offer no satisfactory answer. He stopped walking and looked at her, trying to fight the sense of panic that welled up inside when he confronted how little control, he had over the direction of his life. "I already called Andrew Card before you came down." "Good, that's what you should do."

"It's not the first time I've called him since... everything happened. It's the fourth or fifth, but he hasn't returned my calls."

"He's busy tying up loose ends. Calling Card is the right thing. I just don't think you should try to get involved any further, at least alone."

"What do I do if Card doesn't call back, or when he finally does, he tells me he can't do anything?"

"There's nothing you can do, either. Neither you nor I have the resources to go flying around the world, and even if we did, we don't have the knowledge or the authority to do anything." She paused. "What do you think would happen if you ended up killing a bunch of Coven leaders outside the country? They'd toss you in jail and throw away the key."

John nodded. "I think it's strange that they haven't done it here, don't you? Five important people have vanished."

Amy glanced around, making sure the sidewalk was empty. "But they haven't found any bodies," she whispered. "There's no proof a crime has been committed. That's the reason Card hasn't called you back. It's his way of telling you your involvement is over where the Coven is concerned, and you should keep your mouth shut and lie low for a while."

"Even though they could be torturing and murdering other people? And we haven't talked about this, but what about Jessica Lodge? What am I supposed to do about her? She's related to all of this you know."

"We *think*."

"Well, I *think* this girl was in England, and I *think* that's where Jessica is, as well."

"You think this girl has something to do with Jessica?" "Maybe as a victim."

"Why do you think that?"

John was starting to get frustrated with her questions, but he was trying not to show it. He knew she really didn't believe him, and he realized they were close to having their first fight as a couple. "Because" he said, biting off the words, "Jessica went to Cornwall on her last trip. She didn't tell any of us, but Rich Harvey knew. He let it slip one day when we were at lunch. I didn't think anything about it at the time. Only later, when I knew he was part of the Coven, it seemed more significant."

She looked at him, and her face softened. "I know how you feel. I just think that after everything we've been through, we deserve a little break. And..."

"And what?" he demanded.

"You ought to hear yourself. What you're describing isn't a story, it's just guesses and intuition, and it's coming in the aftermath of a huge shock to your system. It isn't anything you would pursue if somebody else told you this stuff."

He stopped walking and turned to face her. "Two weeks ago, I was a rational reporter who always followed the rules. I checked my sources, and I always verified the facts." He paused. "But then this woman's spirit started talking to me, taking me places, pointing things out to me. It seemed crazy because I didn't believe in stuff like that, but the fact that she talked to me, and I listened made it possible for us to stop a chain of horrible murders that had been going on around here for over three hundred years. And it made it possible for me to save your life."

Amy nodded. "Yes, but now I think we should let other people—"

"What if my dream was another message, but a different kind? What if nobody else gets these damn messages? What do I do, ignore them, say they're somebody else's problem? What if there's nobody else that can do anything about it? What would you want me to do if that little girl was your daughter? Think about that. What should I do, Amy? What would *you* do if you were in my shoes?"

Amy shook her head. "I don't know," she said softly.

"Yes, you do."

She reached out suddenly and gripped his arms. "Just please be careful. We got lucky as hell the first time around If you get involved with those people again, you're going to be farther from home and everything will be more dangerous. Promise me you'll be careful."

"I haven't done anything yet, but yes, I promise I'll be careful."

CHAPTER THREE

When John walked into the *Salem News* offices and onto the newsroom floor, he looked across the room through the glass walls of his office and spotted a stranger sitting in one of the visitor's chairs. The man looked to be in his fifties, with short gray hair and a dark suit, but he didn't look familiar. John glanced at several of the early arriving staffers to see if anyone was going to speak up and tell him why one of them had told a stranger it was okay to take a seat in his office when he wasn't even there; however, everyone he made eye contact with shrugged and shook their head.

"He was already here when we got here," one of them offered.

"He was already inside the building?" John demanded.

"Yeah."

"How the hell did he get a key?" "He said Mrs. Lodge gave him one."

"We'll see about that," he snapped and strode quickly toward his office.

"Can I help you?" he said in a curt voice when he came to his office door.

The man turned and gave him an appraising look as he stood. "Chester Cabot," he said, holding out a business card. John noticed that his shirt was very white and perfectly stiff with starch, his burgundy tie redolent of power but not over- stated, his pants flawlessly pressed, his black shoes shined to a mirror finish.

John took the card as he went past Cabot to take a seat behind his desk. Without looking at it, he eyed Cabot. The man seemed cool and unruffled and very sure of himself. "Most people wait out in the lobby and only come in here when they're invited."

"I was invited."

"By whom?" John demanded, even though he was quite sure he already knew.

"Your employer, Mrs. Jessica Lodge."

John finally glanced down at the card, which said that Cabot was a partner at the law firm of Cabot, Cabot, and Pilkington. It was a name John knew well, one of the whitest of all the white shoe law firms in Boston whose clients were known for their blue blood and deep pockets and whose partners were known for their equally blue blood, their professional discretion, and their intelligence. "I see.

What do you want with me, Mr. Cabot."

Cabot leaned down and removed a sheet of letterhead stationery from a briefcase that stood beside is chair. He handed it across. "Mrs. Lodge has issued us instructions to shut down this paper on her behalf."

John stared at the man for a long silence because his brain seemed to freeze. The lawyer stared back, appearing unfazed by the news he had just delivered. John finally managed to ask, "May I ask the reasons she has made this decision now?" "I can only surmise that it is because the paper has been losing money for some time."

"It's also been Mrs. Lodge's favorite investment."

Cabot drew himself a little more upright. "Nothing stays a favorite forever, it appears. However, I cannot speculate any further on her motives or the reason for her change of heart. I am just here to see that her instructions are carried out.

"I assume the employees will be given reasonable severance."

Cabot reached down and withdrew a file folder with a bound document inside. "This will lay out the terms of each person's severance. You will note that each person is being offered two years' salary at their present compensation if they sign a non-compete agreement." He handed the document across to John. "Please read this and let me know if you have any questions."

Although Jessica's offer was extremely generous in dollars, John looked at Cabot in amazement. "She's shutting down the paper, but she wants people to sign a non- compete. That's crazy! Are you saying she doesn't want a paper to exist in Salem?"

Cabot cleared his throat. "Again, I am simply here to execute her orders and deliver her offer. I cannot and will not guess what her motives are. We will expect the agreements signed and the offices vacated by Friday."

"This coming Friday? Today's Monday. That's only five days."

"I am aware."

"What about the printing equipment, the computers?" "Mrs. Lodge will keep every-thing. It's all explained in
the document."

John looked through the glass walls of his office at the newsroom and the staffers who were already hard at work. Twenty-four people worked at the *Salem News*, twenty-four people who would be out of their jobs this coming Friday. "I haven't read the fine print yet, but I'll hazard a guess," John said. "Everyone gets their severance as long as they don't go to work for another paper within say, a hundred miles, *and* if they refrain from writing about several disappearances that took place in this city just about a week ago."

Cabot just looked at him and didn't answer.

"Bingo," John said, "I hit it right on the nose, didn't I?" Cabot still did not respond.

"Let me ask you one more question before you leave, Mr. Cabot. How do you feel right now? Do you feel good about yourself?"

"That has no bearing on the matter at hand."

"Sure, it does. Five longtime citizens of this town disappeared, and another person killed himself. I believe the five people who disappeared are dead, and I *know* that there are unseemly truths that need to become known, about why they died and how they died, and the things they did while they were alive that no one knows about. Mrs. Lodge doesn't want those stories told, and you are abetting Mrs. Lodge's attempt to make sure those truths never see the light of day. How you feel about the fact that you are covering up terrible crimes is particularly important."

Cabot stood and picked up his briefcase. "Out by Friday, Mr. Andrews. Sign the agreement in the bound document if you wish to receive more than the minimum severance dictated by law. Good day."

Cabot turned and walked out. As John watched him make his way through the newsroom, he felt a fresh flash of paranoia and wondered whether Cabot was just a hired gun with a leathery, dead heart, or whether he was another member of the Coven, someone outwardly wealthy and successful in his own right yet secretly involved in Devil worship and blood sacrifice. There was no way to know, he realized, short of breaking into another Coven meeting and finding Cabot at the table.

For half a second he wished he were looking at Cabot's back through the scope of a gun, and as soon as the thought surfaced, he sat up and gave his head a shake. That was exactly the way he could not afford to think. Paranoid reactions would eventually make him into a vigilante, one who shot first and asked questions later and found a way to forgive himself for the innocents who got in the way of the "cleansing" process. No, as hard as it was going to be, he had to continue to think like a journalist, and that meant getting the facts, the *real* facts, and not acting until he had them, even if those facts dealt with things that the world would view with utter skepticism.

He turned and saw Amy giving him a questioning look, and he signaled for her to come into his office. "What was that about?" she asked as she stepped inside.

"Let's get everyone together at ten a.m. for an announcement," he said, his voice terse with anger. "We're being shut down, effective Friday."

CHAPTER FOUR

By eight o'clock that evening, after he had spoken to the entire staff, given them the bad news and dealt as well as he could with their mixture of stunned anger and tears and confusion, and then somehow managed to coax them to put out that day's edition, John sat in his office and looked out at the empty newsroom. Amy was the only other person still there, and when she saw him looking around, she got up, came into his office, and gave him a sad smile.

"Buy you a drink?" "How about ten drinks?"

She smiled and jerked her head. "Come on, let's get out of here."

He stood and they walked out together and through the dark streets. Amy buttoned her coat against the damp chill of the evening, and then she put her arm through John's and drew close to him. Her warmth and the scent of her perfume helped bring him back to the present. "Jesus," he muttered, "the past week has really knocked me for a loop."

"It's knocked both of us for a loop." "I'm just glad you're with me," he said. "Me too."

They went in silence for another couple blocks and walked into Victoria Station. Amy led John to a corner table near the back and when the server came over, she ordered two Hendrick's martinis, straight up with lemon twists. She handed a glass to John and then raised hers in a toast.

"Here's to the next leg of our adventure."

John raised his own glass. "Let me amend that. Here's to a quiet, boring life for a while." He smiled and took a long pull, feeling the wonderful burn as the gin went down his throat.

He realized with a fitting sense of irony that his distress at the announcement of the paper's closing had begun to jar him from the shellshock of having killed five people and narrowly saving Amy's life and his own. At the same time, he realized that as much as the past week had been about welcome numbness, it was a luxury he could no longer afford.

Up until then, the numbness had been necessary. It had helped him get past the violence and horror of the night in the Coven's catacombs, and his grief at discovering that the Coven had been responsible for the car accident years earlier that claimed his wife's life, and for the years of betrayal when his ostensible friend, Rich Harvey, had actually been a member of the Coven. As much as he had needed the numbness, the announcement of the paper's closing now required him to have his senses engaged. He needed to be aware, to feel every bit of what was going on now. Deep down, what he was feeling was rage.

He couldn't yet prove that Jessica Lodge was the seventh member of the Coven, the leader known as the Inquisitor, but in his gut, he was certain of it; however, right then, he wanted something else even more. He wanted to confront her, to look her in the eye and force her to tell him why she had *really* destroyed the paper that for so many years had mattered more to her than all the other companies in her family's vast corporate portfolio.

At no point in the past had profit been the slightest motivation where the *Salem News* was concerned. Jessica Lodge had loved that paper, at least assuming the things he thought he knew about her were anything but a network of carefully fashioned lies. Now he wanted to confront her and force her to acknowledge the hurt she had brought to so many people who had worked so long and tirelessly for her paper.

He took another long pull of his martini, looked down at the mostly empty glass, and signaled to the server to bring him another then raised his glass. "The next leg of our adventure."

"You sound like you already know what it's going to be." "I do. Is your passport up to date?"

Her eyes became cautious, but she nodded.

"Good, I think we need to go to England."

"Why?"

"I'm going to find that bitch and make her tell me why she's really closing the paper."

"What good is that going to do? We both know why she's doing it."

"Because she doesn't want anybody writing about the other members of the Coven and digging into the topic of Devil worship in Salem and other places. And the reason she doesn't want it is because she's involved in the Coven up to her armpits, and she doesn't want to ruin her good name."

"As much as I know you want to get back at her, we've got enough on our plates right here. We've got to get the paper closed by Friday and help everyone figure out what they're going to do next."

"And what are we supposed to do after Friday?" Amy looked down at her glass and shook he head.

"We can't just take this lying down." John went on, "Did you read the agreement she wants everyone to sign? The whole point is to keep us from finding the truth, I for one will get this story out to the public and won't stop until I do."

The server brought his second martini, and John drained the rest of his first drink, handed her the glass, and took an immediate hit on his second.

Amy's lips were pressed in a tight line, and he could see that she wanted to argue. Before she had a chance to open her mouth, John's cell phone rang. He took it from his pocket and glanced at the caller ID. Seeing it was Andrew Card, he hit the answer button.

"Well, look who's finally getting back," he said. "Well, hello to you, too."

"Where have you been?"

"Traveling," he said, offering no further details. "Have you heard the news?"

"What news?"

"Jessica Lodge is closing the paper. Friday is our last edition, then everyone is cut loose. She's offered two-year's salary if no one works for another paper within a hundred miles of Salem and if nobody writes anything about certain 'rumored disappearances' that occurred a week ago." "I'm sorry to hear that, but how do you expect me to help?"

"Jessica Lodge has left the country. I want to find her."

There was a long silence, then Card said, "Not a good idea."

John ignored the comment and plowed ahead. "That day I took you underground to the Coven's meeting room and their sacrifice chamber, you said something about Covens— plural, as in more than one."

"Did I?"

"Yeah, you implied it was an international problem." There was another long silence.

"Anyway, I'm assuming Jessica is in contact with another Coven, and I'm assuming it's in England because she spends so much time over there. I just thought I'd let you know that I'm going to head over there and see if you might be able to help me find her."

Beside him Amy started shaking her head.

"There may be a time for this later on, but it's not now," Card said. "It would be better to wait until some other things get lined up, until some other people are in a better position to help you. If you go over now, by yourself, you'll be getting into something much bigger and nastier than you realize."

"Bigger and nastier than what I saw that night in the cata- combs?"

"Maybe."

He pushed ahead, ignoring his fear, his reporter's instincts telling him Card wanted to intimidate him. "How about helping me with a few more details. Like whom are these 'people' you just referred to? How long am I supposed to wait until they're 'in a position to help' me?"

"I'm sorry I can't be any more specific, but I am urging you to be patient."

"What if I can't wait?"

"Then I'll probably go to your funeral, and that would be a terrible waste."

"Is that a threat?"

"Of course not. I'm just trying to tell you you're making a terrible mistake trying to take this any further on your own right now. People are working on this problem, people who will be your allies. You have to trust me on that."

John was silent. He looked across the table at Amy and

saw the worry and frustration in her eyes.

"Okay," he said into the phone. "I'll think about it." "Don't think about it, just do it. Please, for everyone's

sake."

John killed the call and looked at Amy. "Card's in your camp. It seems like everyone wants me to leave this alone."

She nodded, but before she could say anything, he reached across the table and took her hands in his, careful not to squeeze too hard where the cuts on her palms were still healing. "I know the *Salem News* is just a small city newspaper. We're not *The New York Times* or *The Washington Post*. We report on the school board and the city council meetings and high school games and road repairs and local politics. But at the same time, people who engaged in unspeakable acts of evil have betrayed this community. You *saw* it. You were there. You understand what we're dealing with."

Amy squeezed his fingers hard. "And that's exactly where we need to focus our energy. Right here, not go on a wild goose chase to England. You think I'm supposed to be braver than that and more intrepid and willing to go find Jessica Lodge and another Coven in

England, but right now, I'm not. The pictures in my brain are just too horrible for me to go chasing after those people. I still see those two dead kids hanging from the wall and Cabby Corwin sticking that scalpel into my palms. I'm sorry, but we need to worry about this community first."

John struggled to swallow his impatience, because in a calm and more rational part of his mind, he had to acknowledge she was right. He nodded. "Sure," he said.

"Besides," she said, looking up from the table and smiling, "there are two other things we need to focus on."

"What are those?"

"We need to talk to Sarah."

John tensed slightly. His twenty-eight-year-old daughter was not happy that John was romantically involved with a woman only eight years older than herself, and she had let her feelings be known. Sarah could be hardheaded and judgmental, and talking to her was something that could easily turn into a confrontation if not managed properly. Even though he wasn't eager to take that risk, after a second he nodded, reminding himself that underneath her hard shell Sarah was warm and caring, and they had always enjoyed a wonderful relationship.

Amy was right. He wanted and needed to do everything he could to keep their relationship strong. However, on the other hand he *had* been a widower for over four years now, and part of him expected Sarah to accept the fact he was a human being with human needs. Sarah needed to let him live his life and just get on with her own. However, even as he thought this it occurred to him that calling his daughter rigid and judgmental was like the pot calling the kettle black.

"Okay," he agreed. "I'll call her when we leave here and ask her to dinner tomorrow." He looked at Amy and a smile began to work its way up his face. "What was the other thing?"

"Well, I was thinking of a little adult physical contact."

John felt the warmth in his eyes spread all the way to the region beneath his belt. "When would you like to make that happen?"

"Are you done drinking martinis?"

He thought for a second then shook his head. He was still upset that they were shutting the paper down. "I think I need at least one more."

"Then how about tomorrow night?" "After Sarah leaves? Excellent idea."

"I'm glad you don't think it would be a good idea to do it while she's there."

"Somehow I don't think she'd take it in the right spirit."

"No."

CHAPTER FIVE

John The next morning, nursing a biting hangover John walked into the newsroom only to realize that the entire staff had gotten there before him. They gathered around one of the desks in the middle of the room, and they turned as a group as he walked in.

"Got a minute?" asked Jefferson Daniels. He was one of the longtime reporters, in his fifties, heavyset, and mostly bald with a band of gray hair along the sides. His laugh was loud and infectious. He was well liked and trusted by the other staffers. With the last name of Daniels and the telltale red nose and broken blood veins of a serious drinker, every- one knew him as Jack.

John glanced up at the clock and saw that it wasn't even eight o'clock. He shrugged. "Sure." Jack Daniels glanced back at the others, and they nodded for him to go ahead. "We've been talking," he began. "We know we get a lot more money if we sign the non-compete agreement."

"A *lot* more," John echoed.

"But, I mean, we're also newspaper people, right? What're we gonna do if we want to stay in Salem but we can't work for another paper?"

Lucinda Jenkins, a heavyset matronly woman who had run the front desk and answered the phones for over twenty years, nodded. "Personally, I don't want to work at Walmart."

"They wouldn't hire you at Walmart," quipped Jack Daniels. "You're too rude. You'd scare away their customers."

"Only if they looked like you, you worthless old Irish drunk."

"Flattery will get you nowhere."

Bert Hagstrom, a short man with the bristly gray hair of a hedgehog, the belly of a professional beer drinker, and the arms of a stevedore, also nodded. Bert was running the printing presses and every other mechanical thing at the paper for the same number of years that Lucinda had run the front desk. "What the hell am I gonna do if I can't play around with these stupid machines?"

"You could always try playing with yourself, but that equipment probably doesn't work any better than your printers," Jack Daniels added.

A handful of people chucked, but there were grumbles.

"What are you saying?" John asked.

"A bunch of us don't want to sign. Our wives work, our kids are out of college, and we've all got a few bucks put away. The others can't afford to turn down the money, and we old guys are stubborn and stupid," piped Jack Daniels. "We think in general you're a lousy editor who can barely put enough words together to order lunch. You're also a horrible person to work for, but we figure the evil we know is better than the evil we don't. If you'll do it with us, we want to buy the building and the printing presses and put out our own paper."

John looked at the small group. Behind Daniels's joking demeanor, which was the only way the man ever expressed anything, he knew the old reporter was dead serious, and that meant the others were, as well. "I have to tell you I'm pretty sure the building and presses won't be for sale," John said. "I don't think Mrs. Lodge wants us putting out a paper. I think that's the whole point."

"What's the old bag got to hide?"

John ran his tongue around the inside of his mouth. He glanced at Amy out of the corner of his eye, and he saw her give him a nod. "Um, it's possible that what she has to hide is so strange that reporting on it will make this paper sound like the *National Enquirer*."

Jack Daniels nodded. "I've felt for a long time we've been forced to write news readers already know about. We've never been able to write about two-headed babies or haunted buildings or UFOs or Elvis sightings. Think about how many more papers we would have sold."

"Think what you would have been like before you rotted your brains with booze," Hagstrom said.

Jack Daniels gave him a wicked smile. "Not nearly as charming." He grew serious and turned to John. "We've all heard a few rumors about Jessica, so we know whatever the truth is it might be pretty weird. I don't think any of us are afraid to report on anything that happens in this town. Everybody else agree?"

The other all nodded their assent.

"You're saying you don't care about money, and you don't care if you sound like a bunch of crackpots," John asked.

"I've always sounded like a crackpot," Jack said, "so I'm in."

"We're all in," Tim Monahan said. He was a tall, cadaverous reporter who had been at the paper for ten years, and before then had spent thirty years in a storied career at *The Boston Globe*. "There are nine of us all together. Me and Jack can do the reporting on the days Jack's sober. The other days I'll do it alone."

"That'll be Monday and Thursday I'll be helping out," Jack said. "That is if I have to be sober."

"Jackie can do the ad sales," Monahan went on, nodding toward Jackie McKinny, another veteran, and the best of the three-person ad sales staff. "Bert will keep everything running just the way he always has, and Lucinda will keep us all straight." He went through a couple other key positions, and John realized that, along with Amy and himself, they had all the major holes filled.

"So, are you with us, you worthless sonofabitch?" Jack Daniels asked. He looked at Amy, "We, of course, would like you to join us, as well. But we also realize you're a bit younger than this group of fossils and you may need the money."

Amy smiled and nodded. "I think I could be persuaded."

Daniels's expression became serious. "It's a lot of security to give up."

"It's Jessica's money. She's trying to buy our silence." "Then we're proud to have you," Daniels said. He looked

at John again. "Well?"

John wondered if her willingness reflected a rekindled sense of spirit or a hope that getting the two of them involved in a new daily paper would keep him close to home and not running off to track down Jessica Lodge. Either way, it didn't matter because he was in with both feet. He looked at the staffers standing in front of him and felt his eyes burn with tears of pride and gratitude. He blinked to get things under control then nodded. "I'm in."

"Well, don't get all emotional about it," Jack Daniels grumbled as he started walking away. "We got a goddamn paper to get out."

John turned and went into his office, his mood suddenly far more buoyant than he would have thought possible earlier. An hour later he had spoken to Sarah, reiterating the dinner invitation he had left on her voice mail the previous evening. She agreed to come over that night at seven. He had also contacted Chester Cabot who confirmed that neither the building in which the paper was found, nor the printing presses would be offered for sale, although the paper would no longer be publishing.

"Am I to interpret these questions as an indication you intend to continue publishing some sort of paper independently?" Cabot asked.

"That's probably a reasonable assumption."

"Everyone who chooses to do this will be leaving quite a bit of money on the table. You included."

"We are all able to do the math."

"So be it. My client has asked me to advise you that we will adhere very strictly to the laws relating to libel and defamation of character, should you attempt to try and seek vengeance via the press."

"Thanks for the *advice*."

John did his best to ignore his hangover and spent the rest of the day working with half his staff to put out a paper with a smaller number of articles than usual because the other half of the staff, including Amy, were involved in trying to lease computers and office furniture, as well as secure guaranteed printing contracts and office space. By the end of the day, they had found a small, free weekly paper that was available in most shops and restaurants that targeted the tourist market. The paper's management was delighted to pick up a contract to print their daily circulation. Amy found a space in a recently renovated warehouse a little way from the heart of Salem that could be had for much less rent than was available in the city center.

By the time he left the office for the evening, John had started to think setting up a new paper and keeping their old subscription base was not only possible, but it was also starting to appear very doable. It made him feel good that, in at least a small way, he was getting back at Jessica Lodge, because the people who put out the *Salem News*, day after day, year after year, weren't going to let the paper go out of business.

Amy had left a little earlier because she needed to shop for their upcoming dinner with Sarah. John finished-up, said goodnight to the last of the folks left in the newsroom then went to a wine shop. He bought three bottles of La Crema Chardonnay and two bottles of well-aged Oregon Pinot Noir. By the time he walked into his house, Amy had water boiling and a pile of vegetables on a chopping board.

"What are we having?"

"Veal chops and ratatouille. You want to start the grill as soon as you change your clothes?"

John put the Chardonnay in the refrigerator and the Burgundies on the counter then went up to slip into blue jeans. A minute later he was back downstairs where he opened one of the chardonnays and poured a glass for himself and one for Amy.

"Let's hope this goes well," he said, clicking his glass gently to hers.

"Have faith in your daughter."

"I do, but..." Instead of finishing the thought he went outside, put charcoal in the grill, and lit it. Most of his neighbors had gas grills, but John was stubbornly old fashioned and stuck to his time-honored tradition of real coals.

He tried to shove down the nervous tremor that churned through his guts as he thought about the last conversation, he'd had with Sarah in which Amy was the topic. What was that Sarah had said? *"It would be nice if you picked somebody a little closer to your age. She could be my sister."* Yes, that was it exactly. How was Sarah going to react tonight? He wanted to share Amy's faith in Sarah, but he didn't have a good feeling.

CHAPTER SIX

As he waited for his coals to light, John paced around the house. Sarah had extremely early hours in the morning for her news show, so she tended to arrive early and leave early so she could get to bed. It was part of his daughter's rigidity. She kept to her schedule and didn't deviate. In her personal life she liked hard walls and black-and-white opinions, strange for a TV news journalist whose profession required dealing with issues colored in constantly shifting shades of gray, he thought.

But even as he thought this, he realized he was wrong. Sarah was perfect for the FOX News affiliate where she worked. Unlike his, her politics were right wing, and she and her co-workers loved absolute positions, like the fact that older widowers shouldn't fall in love with younger women. John sipped his Chardonnay, told himself he shouldn't have any more, but took another sip anyway and drained the glass. To keep himself from going into the kitchen for more wine, he straightened the pillows and peeked out the front curtains a couple times.

On one pass by the front window, he saw someone who looked like they were hurrying away from his front door, and for half a second he wondered if it was Sarah. Had she lost her nerve and walked away? As soon as he thought it, he decided no. The person he had seen had been too big, a man certainly. Besides, Sarah wasn't going to lose her nerve. That wasn't her style. More likely she would come in with her barrels loaded with buckshot and pull both triggers at once, verbally of course.

John looked at his watch. Five past seven. Okay, for once in her life Sarah was late. She was caught in traffic, that must be it. Thinking about it that way made him realize the stakes were huge. He wanted his relationship with his daughter as well as his relationship with Amy. He just hoped he could work things out with Sarah so he could have both.

At fifteen after seven he gave up and went to the kitchen and poured himself more wine. Sipping it, he started to pace harder, his nervousness tinged with worry.

"Take it easy," Amy said in a calming voice. "It's all going to work out okay."

"Yeah," John said, but he wasn't convinced. If Sarah was going to be this late, it was strange she hadn't called. What if she'd been in a car accident? He tried to wall off the memories of the other night he had paced like this—the night Julie had gone out in a rainstorm to pick up the wine for a party they were hosting. It had been the night she died in the accident, the night, as he learned much later, the Coven had murdered her because they had thought John was driving the car.

He looked out the window again, relieved to see the pavement was dry, the sky perfectly clear. He dug his cell phone from his pocket and checked the battery, and it was at 96 percent, and then looked at the ringer to make sure the ringer was on. There were no missed phone call or text messages.

At twenty-five past he went into the kitchen. "I'm really getting worried. This isn't like Sarah."

"Have you called her?"

John shook his head as he dug his phone from his pocket and pressed Sarah's number on his speed dial list. He listened as the call went through and the line began to ring. When her message came on, he killed the call.

"John, she's about to have an awkward dinner with her father and his lover, a woman who is much younger than her mother was. You like to believe Sarah has brass balls; but she may be outside sitting in her car trying to work up the nerve to come to the door."

John nodded, relieved that Amy was thinking in logical emotional terms and not traffic accident terms. He went to the front door, put his wine glass on the side table, and

opened the door. An envelope rested on the doormat at his feet. It was small and square, the kind used for invitations. It was addressed to "John Andrews," and underneath it read, "By Hand."

Curious, he picked it up, stepped back inside, and closed the door. He slipped his finger under the flap and removed the stiff note card inside. On the card, written in lovely calligraphy were the four words: "She is with us." Below the words was a carefully drawn symbol that drew his eyes like iron shavings racing to a magnet: a pentagram.

John closed his eyes and grabbed his chest, feeling the world spin around him. Was this sick bastard's idea of a joke? He fervently hoped it was because he couldn't deal with the idea, he was reentering the nightmare from which he had escaped barely a week earlier.

The pentagram had been the Coven's symbol. It was on the grave markers of the Coven's original members. The graves at Gallows Hill of those founders of Salem's first Coven formed a pentagram, although the symbol was so well hidden among the other family gravestones in Harmony Grove Cemetery John had only been able to see it when the spirit of Sarah Nurse had made the gravestones glow.

John shook his head to try and clear his thoughts. Okay, he told himself, if this was a joke, the jerk who'd put the envelope here was waiting around to see what kind of affect it might have. The rage he felt was empowering. It helped push away the other possibilities, the ones he could not bear to think about. He remembered the person he had seen hurrying away from his front door over thirty minutes earlier. That had to be the one who put the envelope on his steps.

Stepping back outside, John looked up and down Pickering Wharf for any sign of the man, but the sidewalk was empty. He pulled the door closed behind him and started right; in the direction he had seen the man walking. He went fast, his pace just short of a run, and tried to remember what the person had looked like: big shoulders, six feet tall, and walked with a bit of a stoop. He wore a hat, so he didn't see his face or hair.

Thinking he would remember the coat if he saw it again from the back, he headed down to the corner, intending to go into a couple of the nearest bars and see if somebody who fit that description might be standing at the bar regaling his friends with the story of the great practical joke he had just pulled on John Andrews.

He was walking fast, so immersed in his rage that he almost missed the car. It was a Toyota Celica, dark green, just like Sarah's. He stopped, walked over, and looked at the car more closely to see if anyone was behind the wheel. The car was empty, but when he put his hand on the hood, he could feel the engine heat still coming up through the metal. It meant the car hadn't been here long.

He walked around to the back bumper and caught sight of Sarah's telltale bumper stickers, one for Romney/Ryan and another for FOX News, and fear and helplessness quickly eroded his rage. His brain sparked with unconnected thoughts, all of them aimed at finding a hope, a rationalization, to believe his world wasn't coming apart again.

When he walked back around to the driver's side door and looked down, whatever hope he'd been able to muster vaporized instantly. On the ground just beside the door, were a set of keys and a cell phone. Dreading what he knew he was going to find, he took out his own cell phone, hit her number, and watched the phone on the pavement light up and start to vibrate.

He flicked on the flashlight app on his phone and shined it through the side window. As if they had left the car keys on the ground for him to find so there would be no doubt in his mind, he saw another envelope on the driver's seat similar in size to the one he'd found on his doorstep.

This envelope addressed the same way as the first. He picked up her keys, he clicked the locks and grabbed the envelope. The same calligraphy graced the note inside. This time it said: "Stop. Last Warning." Beneath it, like a perverse signature, was the pentagram.

CHAPTER SEVEN

John and Amy huddled at the kitchen table in John's house staring at the two pentagram note cards. John had a mug of hot coffee cupped in his hands, and he kept shaking his head as if by doing so he could deny the reality of this moment.

"They're not gone," he whispered. "I mean, I knew they weren't, but with their leaders all dead, I thought they would be in retreat. I thought it would take time for them to get organized, but it didn't and now they've got Sarah."

He stumbled back into the house, barely able to put coherent thoughts together. He tried to tell Amy what he'd found. She sat him down at the table and gave him a coffee while they tried to calm down enough to decide what to do.

"Come on, John, we've got to think and come up with a plan," she coaxed.

John rocked in his chair, bombarded by guilt and fear. "You know what they do to people," he said through gritted teeth.

"I also know you beat them once. That means you can do it again."

"I don't know." As he said it, he closed his eyes and thought back over the previous weeks when the spirit of Rebecca Nurse had led him into the heart of the Coven and how the power, she had somehow infused in him had allowed him to destroy them. The results had been horrible, bloody beyond words, worse than the damage from a pointblank shot from twelve-gauge shotgun, but the leaders killed. Cabby Corwin, The Very Reverend Staunton Winthrop, Senator Austin Howell, Amanda Putnam Pendergast, Abigail Putnam, all of them dead at his hand. It had been final, over, done. Even the lurid burn marks on his left forearm that had appeared after his first encounter with Rebecca Nurse and that had forced him to confront the reality of the Coven had disappeared.

It had taken every ounce of strength and courage he had to endure the past couple of weeks. He thought back to how weakened Amy had admitted to being, and he realized he had been kidding himself when he'd proposed going to England to chase after Jessica Lodge. He was still close to his own limits. He needed to rest and regain his mental and physical strength, only now, there would be no opportunity.

He grabbed handfuls of his hair and pulled. First his wife, and now his daughter, and even worse he had no idea who "they" were. That realization brought a fresh bolt of paranoia. They could be his neighbors, someone at the news- paper, anyone he passed on the street. Hadn't one of his erstwhile best friends, Rich Harvey, also been a senior member of the Coven?

And why had they taken Sarah now? Did they know about the plans to restart the paper? Did they know about his threat to find Jessica Lodge? Who could have been behind this kidnapping? His first thought was the lawyer, Chester Cabot, but then he thought of the staff at the paper. The honest answer was he had absolutely no idea who he could trust. It was also the reason he couldn't go to the police or anyone else and ask for help. He and Amy were completely on their own.

Amy reached out and gripped his wrist and slowly forced him to unclench his hands and release his hair. As he brought his forearms back down to the table, he looked at the two pentagram cards and shook his head.

"We need help," Amy said.

Under any set of normal circumstances, she would have been right, but nothing about this was normal. He looked up at her. "Who do we call?"

"The police?"

All John could think about was that Cabby Corwin had been a detective on the Salem police, and he had also been one of the leaders of the Salem Coven. "How can we trust them?"

Amy nodded. "What about that one policeman you know?" "Andrew Card?" John shook his head. "I made the mis- take of telling him I wanted to go to England to find Jessica

Lodge. I doubt he'll even return my call." "John, you said that you thought he was part of a group that's hunting the Coven internationally. Remember?"

John nodded. "It wasn't so much what he said as what he implied. Or at least what I chose to read into it. He's stingy with the facts."

"Call him. Tell him what happened and ask him what we should do."

John dug out his cell phone and called Card's number. When he got the recording he said, "The Coven has taken my daughter. Call me as soon as possible."

He looked up at Amy and shook his head. "Now what?" "He works for the state police, right? Call their headquarters and talk to Card's superior. Tell him you need to speak with Card, that it's a matter of life and death."

John nodded; grateful she was telling him what to do when his own brain was filled with molasses. He searched his web browser then called the state headquarters in Framingham. A desk sergeant answered. John explained that he needed to get a message to a senior member of the state police detective unit.

"I'll put you through to Captain Rothstein's extension, sir. His secretary has gone for the evening, so you'll have to leave a message."

"Can I speak to somebody right now?"

"Is this an emergency, sir? If it is, you need to call 911."

John ground his knuckles into his eyes, trying to keep his voice under control. The last thing he wanted was the entire Massachusetts State Police and the FBI descending on a kidnapping, at least he didn't want that before he'd had a chance to speak with Card. "No, it's not an emergency. It's important that I speak to Captain Rothstein as soon as possible."

"Hold on, please."

A second later John heard the recording of Rothstein's assistant asking the caller to leave a detailed message. "This is John Andrews of Salem. I am the executive editor of the *Salem News*. I'm trying to reach Captain Andrew Card on a matter of foremost importance, and I would like to ask that you make sure he returns this call." John left his home, office, and cell numbers, as well as his address.

When he hung up, he looked across at Amy. "I don't know who else to call."

Amy shook her head and gripped his hand. After a second John pushed his chair back from the table and stood. "There is one more person I need to speak with," he said. He walked over to the counter, took a glass from the cabinet, poured himself a stiff bourbon, and then walked to the living room and turned on the lights.

"Okay," he said to Rebecca Nurse's portrait. "I know you've gone to the great beyond someplace, and I have no right so say that you don't deserve your rest after so many years of waiting for your revenge. But I have to tell you that my daughter, Sarah, who is also your direct descendant, was taken by the Coven this evening.

"I don't know what they want with her or what they plan to do." At this he took a deep pull on the bourbon and felt it burn down his throat. "I don't have any idea who these people are. We killed their leaders, but there are clearly more of them around. I don't know if there are any other spirits who are waiting to get even with the Coven, but if you hear this, could you let them know I need help."

John looked up at the cracked oil painting of the old woman sitting in a rocking chair doing her embroidery. Part of him felt like a fool for talking to an ancient portrait, but he knew the strength of Rebecca's spirit because she had infused his body with immense power just a week earlier. The problem was he had no idea how to tap that power, and if he did, whether he would be able to control it, or whether it would even be possible to pull it into his body ever again.

"I really need help," he said, his voice shaking. "Anything you can do would be greatly appreciated."

He was walking back toward the kitchen when his cell phone rang. As he grabbed it and hit the answer button, he saw that the caller's number was blocked. "Hello?" he said, hoping desperately to hear Sarah's voice.

"Daddy?" It *was* Sarah, he realized. His pulse skipped a beat. He heard fear in her tone. His spirit plummeted as quickly as it had soared.

"Sarah!" he said. "Where are you? Are you all right?"

"I don't know where I am. Right now, I'm all right, but I'm scared. The people who took me want me to tell you to leave the Coven alone. They say if you don't," here her voice broke, and he could hear her struggling not to cry. "I don't know what they're talking about, but they say if you don't do what they tell you, you'll never see me again."

"Be brave, Sarah, I'm going to get you out of this," he said, but the call disconnected before his reassuring words could reach his daughter's ears.

He slammed down the phone and reached for his glass of bourbon, finishing the rest in one swallow. "Goddamnit," he shouted. "What the hell am I going to do?"

He had never felt more powerless.

CHAPTER EIGHT

It was the last place in the world he wanted to be, a place that only a week earlier he had promised himself he would never go again, yet here he was, sometime after midnight, having come through an unlocked gate into Harmony Grove Cemetery. The gate was one Rich Harvey had showed him just a week earlier, the night Rich had tried to deliver him to the Coven to be killed.

Overhead, the clouds were low and heavy, threatening rain or even an early snow, but they reflected the lights of the city just enough so that the cemetery's walkways and gravestones were just barely visible. John stood at the bottom of one of the walkways, staring up the hill at the shadowy outline of the Putnam plot, the place where a number of his ancestors on the other side of his family tree had been buried, and the place where a number of the Putnam gravestones formed a well-camouflaged hexagram because, as he had discovered, a number of those same ancestors had been members of the Salem Coven.

He took a deep breath and started up the walkway, toward the Putnam plot and the old granite mausoleum that loomed in the far corner. As he climbed the hill, he could not banish the images that kept coming back to him from the last time he'd been here, scenes from the nightmare abattoir he had found in the vast catacombs beneath the cemetery. He felt drops of cold sweat break from his armpits and run down his sides.

At least he wasn't alone. Even though he had seen the look of utter terror on Amy's face when he told her he needed to come here to try and find Sarah, and even though he would never have asked her to come with him, she'd insisted. It had been more than he could do to make himself return to this horrible place and having Amy with him made it even harder. As much as he despised coming here, he hated even more putting Amy through the stress of returning to a place where she had been shackled to a wall and nearly killed only a few days earlier, but it was the only place in Salem where he thought Sarah's abductors might have brought her. He had no choice but to come here.

They were silent as they walked up the hill. As they approached the front of the mausoleum, a frigid wind seemed to pick up and moan through the leafless branches. He gripped Amy's hand, imagining he could feel a chill seeping into the very marrow of his bones that came from something far more sinister than wind.

Around the back of the mausoleum, the old set of crumbling concrete steps led down to darkness. He took a flashlight from his pocket and shined it down toward the bottom of the steps and the old, rusted door. He heard the breath catch in Amy's throat at the flicker of movement, but it was only the gray tatters of cobwebs in the breeze. Going down the steps, fighting the fear that made him want to turn and run, he led the way to the handprint set into the wall just to the left of the door.

Not letting himself hesitate, because he knew that to delay anything would only intensify his fear, he reached into his pocket and grasped his pocketknife. He fingered open the smallest blade, jabbed the point into the second finger on his left hand, and twisted until he saw a drop of blood. Putting his bloody hand against the indented handprint, he felt the wall soften as if it were greedily drinking in his blood, and a second later he heard the snap of a lock unfastening.

The granite wall to the left of the handprint swung inward, and the terrible darkness beckoned. John aimed his flashlight into the gloom, squeezed Amy's hand for reassurance, and took a step through the opening and into the long lightless tunnel. He let go of Amy's hand, and absently, his fingers went to the pocket of his coat where they wrapped around the checkered wooden grip of the Browning .45 automatic pistol his father had brought back from WWII. He felt the reassuring heaviness and wondered absently if he was going to have to use it.

Without Rebecca Nurse to go with him, he had absolutely no illusions that he would be unable to tap the power he had used the last time he had been here, when he had killed the Coven leaders. Even so, he also knew that he had no compunction whatsoever about killing any member of the Coven he might find here tonight. Having spent his life as a news reporter rather than a newsmaker, he saw this change in himself, this transition from dispassionate observer to cold-hearted killer. He wondered if he should be frightened at what he had become, but he didn't have time to worry.

As soon as he stepped inside the dark opening, lights a little farther down the corridor began to glow. The air in the passage was damp and musty smelling but a strong breeze blew against them, carrying scents of dirt and metal, as if it emanated from someplace very deep in the bowels of the earth. He felt his muscles tighten and felt the stillness of death all around.

Turning off his flashlight, he started to walk through the tunnel with Amy beside him. As if they sensed them coming, more of the wall lights farther along began to glow, just as the ones behind them died out again soon after they went past. Walking through a silence broken only by the scuff of their soles on the stone floor, John tried to let his mind go blank, rejecting the memories of mutilated bodies, both those of victims and Coven leaders, who tried to take over his thoughts.

The walk was exceptionally long, seeming almost endless at certain points. They passed doorways that John had seen but had never tried to open before. Now he stopped at each one, but when he tried them, he found them locked, the handles coated with dust and the metal rusted from long disuse.

The tunnel came to a 'T,' and he knew they had gone a couple hundred yards. He flicked on his flashlight and shined it to the right and seeing that the passage ended in just yards away, he motioned to Amy to turn left.

As they started along the passage, Amy broke the long silence, whispering, "Who built all of this?"

John shook his head, glancing at the smooth stone floor and uniform height and width of the passage. "I don't have any idea."

"Do you think these were originally just a set of caves that people chiseled out?"

John shook his head again. He knew Amy was asking question to try and distract herself from her fear, but he also knew there were so many questions and almost no answers. What was behind the old, rusted doors? John wondered. Someday he needed to come back down here with a crowbar and flashlight—someday when he could stand to reenter this terrible place—and explore every inch of these tunnels and milk them for every bit of information on the Coven that he could glean.

He was doing the same thing Amy was, trying to distract himself from his growing dread, because he recognized the next door they came to, and the sight made the breath catch in his throat. Unlike the other doors they had passed, this one was constructed of thick oak with heavy wrought iron hinges and a stout crossbar that functioned as a lock. The door stood unlocked and slightly ajar, and John eased it open with a toe, half dreading what he might find. Was Sarah in here or had she been in here recently? If she was here, why was the door unlocked? Had they killed her here and left her body?

When the door swung open and he shined his light inside, he blinked in surprise—the room was empty. Just a week earlier, the room was a prison for the Coven's most recent victims. He remembered a filthy blanket crumpled in one corner and a bucket that had reeked of feces a foot or two from the door. Now both items were gone, and the floor had mopped.

They pushed on, going past three similar doors, all of them ajar and all clean and empty. None of them held any sign that a person had recently been held as a prisoner. Ahead, opening another door on the right, he looked in at a bathroom with white tiles on the walls and floor. It too was empty.

Up ahead the passage dead-ended in a door different from all the others. It was a richly polished wood with ornate carvings, in the center of which a demon's head stood out in bas relief. Again, John felt his breathing turn ragged and his pulse kick into high gear as he pictured the room on the other side of the door.

"Do you want to stay here?" he whispered to Amy.

When she said nothing, he turned to glance at her. Her face was pale, and her eyes had a haunted look, but she shook her head no.

Forcing himself to keep moving forward, John grabbed the knob, turned it, and shoved the door inward. The last time he had gone through this door, he had come face to face with the leaders of the Salem Coven and seen an unimaginably gruesome scene.

Unlike the last time he was here, the room was dark, and its silence spoke of emptiness. Even before the lights on the walls came on, he flicked on his flashlight and panned the beam over the gleaming mahogany table, the ornate fireplace mantel against one wall, the polished wood plank floors, and the dark beams across the plaster ceiling. The wall sconces slowly lit the room, and as they did, he heard the breath rasp in Amy's throat and felt her fingers like claws as she gripped his arm.

After another second, his hand now trembling and causing the light to shake, John turned to his left and shined the light into the room that opened just off the underground dining room. Amy whimpered as the flashlight beam lit the room's white tile walls and white tile floor with the large drain in the center, used for sluicing away the blood that pooled after the Coven's sacrifices.

John choked back his own moan because he half expected to see Sarah's body hanging suspended by the shackles in the tile wall. The whole time he had been walking through the underground passage his dread had been building, imagining that he was going to find that his daughter sacrificed like the two young people he had found here the night he saved Amy's life.

Only he saw nothing. The tile walls were clean and white, the tile floor glistening in his flashlight beam, and to his astonishment the shackles were missing from the walls and their screw holes patched with white grout, and there was no sign of Sarah. He stood there breathing heavily, his legs shaking, not sure whether he wanted to cry with relief or collapse in confusion.

He felt Amy's arms come around him as she pulled herself against him and whispered, "Thank God." He could only nod in response, unable to trust his voice.

He turned, walked out of the room, and started to lead the way back down the passage as they retraced their steps and made their way out of the underground lair.

Walking out the unlocked gate at the back of the cemetery and finally climbing into their car, John looked over at Amy. "I really need a drink."

"That makes two of us."

CHAPTER NINE

The next morning having drunk enough bourbon the night before to finally calm down and get himself to sleep, John opened his eyes to an empty bed and a blistering hangover. He slipped on a robe and slippers and stumbled downstairs to find Amy already in the kitchen cooking bacon and eggs. The smell of the food nearly made him lose whatever was in his stomach and he went to the front door, opened it, and stood in the morning wind, shivering, and sucking in breaths of sea-scented air and telling himself he had to quit hammering the booze.

When the wave of nausea passed, he stooped down and picked up that morning's copies of *The New York Times*, *The Wall Street Journal*, and *The Washington Post* and brought them inside.

He took the papers out of their plastic bags and scanned the front pages of each, seeing the world headlines but thinking they were wrong somehow, missing something huge, and that each paper should be trumpeting the tragedy of the previous evening's kidnapping.

Back in the kitchen he collapsed into the same chair he had sat in the previous evening when he'd polished off his bottle of Basil Hayden's, then he fumbled his cell phone from the pocket of his robe and checked for missed phone calls, text messages, or emails. Nothing.

"I called Andrew Card last night, didn't I?" he croaked. "And his boss."

John put his face in his hands. He so much wanted to believe that he could dial her number on the phone and hear her voice, but he knew it wasn't possible. He almost didn't move when his phone started to vibrate. He fished it again from the pocket of his robe, looked at the number, and saw that it was blocked.

He punched the answer button. "Hello?" he said sounding hoarse and excited.

"Mr. Andrews?"

"Yes?"

"This is Captain Steve Rothstein of the Massachusetts State Police. You called me last night on a matter of urgency?"

"Yessir. I've been trying to reach Captain Andrew Card in your organization. I have some valuable information to give him."

"What kind of information?"

"If you don't mind, I'd rather communicate it directly to Captain Card."

"I'm afraid that's going to be difficult."

A sudden cold dread rose in John's stomach. "Did something happen to Captain Card?"

"Not that I'm aware of. The problem is that there is no one by that name in our organization. There was a person with that name, but he left the state police years ago. Are you sure you have the right police force?"

"Massachusetts State Police. That's who he's with. I'm sure of it."

"And you say he's a captain?"

"Yes, I've got his card right here." John went to his wallet where it lay on the counter beside his keys. His hands shook from a combination of his hangover and his sudden fear as he opened the billfold, fished out the now wrinkled card, and read it aloud. "Captain Andrew A. Card. Massachusetts State Police."

"Who gave you that card?"

"The person who claimed it was his."

"I'm sorry to say that there is no such person as Andrew Card on our force at the present time."

John's throat was dry as sand. "Can you please check your records once more? Card may be with a special unit. Maybe he doesn't show up on your roster."

"I checked the entire roster, sir. It sounds like you've had someone impersonating a police officer, which is a serious crime. Now why don't you tell me what this is all about."

John opened his mouth and then closed it again. "I can't," he said and hung up.

John sat in the chair for the next hour, nibbling at a piece of toast and then staring at absolutely nothing, his brain too stunned to even let him move. Amy worked around him in silence, cleaning up the kitchen until she finally dropped into a chair across from him.

"Okay, you're in shock right now. These people have hit you with a Pearl Harbor attack. Your daughter is gone and now you've found out that a man you thought was on your side was an impostor."

John shook his head and tried to focus his eyes on her face. He shook his head as the unorganized thoughts came tumbling out. "How many of these people are there? How do we ever figure out who they are? Are they *everywhere* around us? How do we ever trust anybody?"

"That's exactly what they want. They want you to be afraid to trust. They want you to think there are hundreds or thousands of them, that they're all around us. They're *not*, John. This is a head game. These people are not as strong as they want you to think they are. They worship the Devil. That means they worship entropy and chaos and the end of everything we know. I'm not even sure they under- stand what they're worshipping because I can't imagine why any living creature would worship death. They *can't* be as strong as they're making you think they are. You've got to believe that."

"Then what about Card? Was he one of them, too? And if he was, why did he string me along and want me to believe he was a cop?"

"We don't know the answer. Maybe we never will."

John threw his hands in the air, unable to hold his frustration. "So, what do we do? How do we start to fight? How do we get a clue to where Sarah is?"

"Baby steps. You're going to go upstairs and get into your jogging clothes. You're going to go out and walk or jog for at least an hour. You're not doing yourself or Sarah any good in your current state. You need to get your brain clear. You understand that, right?"

John blinked at her, and he nodded, grateful to have somebody telling him what to do. He stood slowly and went upstairs and came down a couple minutes later in his running pants and a sweatshirt.

"I'll be right here when you get back," Amy said.

John nodded and stumbled out the door. He jogged a couple of blocks to warm up and then started picking up speed. After fifteen minutes he felt heat and oxygen and blood coursing through his body, and he began to feel better. He began pushing hard, not exactly consciously, but imagining he could outrun the guilt and sadness that had nearly paralyzed him and that he could catch the rage he imagined was someplace ahead. He knew his rage was something he desperately needed, a weapon against the weight of fear and uncertainty.

He ran harder and harder, sucking the air deep in his lungs, blowing out what was left of his hangover, feeling stronger and faster as he went. Gradually, and then increasingly, he felt it, his rage starting to boil up from his guts. It was like when Rebecca Nurse's spirit had come into him down in the Coven's underground lair. Rage was power, the denial of fear, the willingness to take risks, the ability to receive pain and endure it so that he could inflict even more on his enemies.

The Coven had told him they had Sarah, and they told him to stop. Stop doing what? Stop restarting the *Salem News*? Stop trying to find Jessica Lodge? It didn't matter what they wanted him to stop. He needed the mouthpiece of a newspaper to fight the Coven when the time came to fight them in print, and he needed to find Jessica Lodge because she had so many of the answers he needed. The Coven might have Sarah, but there was nothing he could do to save her without information and leverage. He knew what the Coven did to the people it captured. Obeying them wasn't a choice because it wasn't going to help Sarah.

Finally understanding what he had to do, he turned for home.

CHAPTER TEN

Back in his house, john went over to Amy and took her in his arms. Holding her tight to his chest, he said, "Thank you for kicking me out of my despondency. For a while there I couldn't think. I couldn't do anything. I was just stuck."

Amy pulled away from him and looked up. "You've taken a huge blow. I don't have a child, but I understand what this means to you. But I also know you're a fighter." She smiled. "You're as good a fighter as I've ever seen, good enough to save my life when I didn't think there was any- thing that could save me. I just want you to know that I'm with you for whatever it takes to get Sarah back, even up to and including a trip to England to get Jessica or whatever else you decide. I've got your back."

John closed his eyes as he felt a hot tear starting to work its way out of the corner of his eye. It felt so extraordinary to have somebody he could depend on; somebody on whom he could really depend. "Thank you," he finally managed, his voice hoarse.

They stayed that way for a long time, and when he finally loosened his embrace and stepped away from her, he had a renewed sense of purpose. "What are you thinking?" she asked. "Starting to have a plan?"

He nodded. "It's sort of a process of elimination." He held up one finger. "I sorely wish Rebecca Nurse were still here, but she's not. No amount of wishing can bring her back.

He held up a second finger. "Of the people we know, there's simply no way to know who we can and can't trust. There just isn't, so we don't trust anybody."

He held up a third finger. "We have no idea where they have taken Sarah. We don't know if she's in Salem, or if she's even in Massachusetts. Heck, we don't even know if she's in the United States."

He held up a fourth finger. "So, in the absence of any living people who can help us, and having no clue where they've taken Sarah, where do we turn? If we can't go forward, we must go backward. We know my ancestors were fighting the Coven exactly the way we are, and I would bet my life we could trust them. Of course, we can't talk to them, so we just have to find out if there are any messages, guides, or clues, they might have left behind that we haven't already found. Let's hope there's something in the past that can help us figure out what the Coven might have done with her." "So, you're heading upstairs?"

He nodded. "The library for starters. I'll go through the house with a fine-toothed comb."

"I'll start on the downstairs," Amy offered. "It'll go faster."

"Deal," John said, recalling that Amy had been the one who found the message from his relative, Captain John Andrews, hidden in the picture frame that held the portrait of Rebecca Nurse. That message had been hugely important in helping them understand that the Coven had been running in Salem for over three hundred years and all that time had been making blood sacrifices to Satan and hunting down and killing anyone who took too much interest in their activities. Thinking about that now and remembering that his own ancestors hadn't been able to trust the people around them any more than he could today, made him feel less alone.

He went upstairs to the home office that had once been the library of Captain John Bancroft Andrews and his other sea captain ancestors who had helped make the Andrews family such a success in early Salem. Through his friendship with Nathaniel Hawthorne and through discoveries made on his own sea voyages, Captain John Bancroft Andrews, like John today, had become deeply concerned about the Salem Coven and its murderous activities. How- ever, unlike his modern-day namesake, Captain Andrews had never been able to tap the power of the spirits of the dead to fight and kill members of the Coven.

John thought about that as he paused in the doorway of his library, taking in the large bay window that overlooked the dark waters of Salem harbor, windows from which his ancestors had been able to look down on their own clip- per ships. He had grown up thinking he had to be in some ways weaker, certainly less intrepid than his forbearers who had gone to sea generation after generation in wooden ships that seemed incredibly small and frail considering the distances they traveled and the savage seas they encountered. He wondered how those old sea captains would view him if they could see the way he had destroyed the leaders of the Coven, and he felt a small flutter of pride that he had acquit-ted himself in a manner that might give those tough old men something to smile about. At least he hoped that might be the case.

He shook off his reverie and focused on the old Hepplewhite mahogany table that stood in the bay window. On top of the table rested a clutter of things from a wide mix of generations: his computer and keyboard; a sextant once used to navigate his family's ships; the leather bound ship's log of the *Formosa*, perhaps the most famous of his family's many clip- per ships; his grandfather's binoculars; an oosik, which was the penile bone of a walrus and had been collected by some enterprising ancestor with a good sense of humor; a wooden model of the *Singapore*, another of his family's ships.

The rest of the room was just as cluttered. A folding Chinese screen stood in one corner; another table held John's own hockey and sailing trophies. The Federal period desk held a stack of unpaid bills, unfiled brokerage and bank statements, and a general confusion of personal documents. The book- shelves sagged with books he had bought and read as well as his aunt's and grandfather's books and leather- bound volumes from the 1800s and even several boxes of old letters and other unbound scraps of writing.

For the next five hours he went through the room, starting to the right of the doorway and working his way around, inch by inch; checking each square of molding and each piece of furniture for hidden compartments; looking to see if ancient messages had been glued to the underside of tables; running his fingers around the edges of the Chinese screen as he felt for bumps or irregularities beneath the fabric.

At his desk he removed each drawer, looked inside and all around the sides and bot- toms, felt the sides of the desk for any hint of a panel that might move, then lay on his back, slid underneath, and looked at the bottom. When he finished, he did the same thing to the Hepplewhite table, but found it as empty of hidden messages as the desk.

He felt along the sides of the fireplace, pushing each slight protuberance in the carved mantel, listening hopefully for the muted click that might show that a hidden panel had opened. When he finally came to the bookshelves, he took each old book, opened it to look for notes written inside the cover, then went through the pages to see if a slip of paper had been carefully inserted somewhere.

He was halfway through when Amy came into the room.

"Nothing downstairs, I'm afraid. I checked every piece of furniture and every single painting, but I came up empty handed. Anything up here?" she asked.

John shook his head. "Totally dry, so far." "Can I help?"

John nodded at the old Andrews family Bible where it lay on the lowest shelf. "You might want to tackle that old beast. I was saving it for last."

The Bible was large, bound with embossed leather, and held together with a metal clasp. Inside, in addition to the Bible itself were blank pages in which births, deaths, and marriages of the Andrews clan had been recorded for over one hundred fifty years. As Amy carried the Bible over to the desk, unfastened the clasp, and laid it open, John went back to the other books.

Coming to a section of ancient leather-bound books that were owned by Captain John Bancroft Andrews, he saw a line of old classics, like *Robinson Crusoe, The Aeneid, The Odyssey, A Pilgrim's Progress, Don Quixote, Pamela,* and *Paradise Lost.* Because the books were old and valuable, he took each one off the shelf with care and turned the pages slowly and gently.

The work was tedious and slow. He had gone through all the books but one and as he started to page through *Paradise Lost,* he began to think there was nothing in the house worth finding, but then a small notation opposite line 422 of Book I caught his eye. It was unusual not so much because of what it said but because there had been no other marginal jotting in any of the other books. Feeling a flutter of excitement, he brought the book over by the window and squinted down at the faded writing.

"Amy, come over here," he said softly.

When she looked over his shoulder at the writing, he glanced at her. "What does that say?"

"I think it says 'Ashtoreth/Astarte equals Elizabeth Turner.'"

"You ever heard of Ashtoreth/Astarte?"

"Ashtoreth and Astarte are sort of synonymous names for a Phoenician goddess who was kind of a sinful love goddess."

He turned all the way around and gaped at her. "How do you know *that*?"

"Too much college, I guess. Some of my unessential and useless knowledge."

"Why is this name in *Paradise Lost*?"

Amy picked up the book and started reading. "Because apparently Ashtoreth was one of the twelve most powerful angels who united with Satan to oppose God."

"Who is Elizabeth Turner?"

Amy went over to John's computer and started an Internet search. After a few minutes of typing, she turned away from the screen. "The best historic local hit is Elizabeth Turner, wife of Captain John Turner."

John snapped his fingers, recognizing the name. "He's the guy who built the first part of what is now known as the House of the Seven Gables."

John picked up *Paradise Lost* again and finished paging through the book. The notation mentioning Ashtoreth/Astarte and Elizabeth Turner seemed to be the only writing he could find. He rubbed his eyes. "This is pretty damn vague. We don't know who wrote this or why they wrote it or when. We don't know whether it means something important or nothing at all. How can we know whether this has anything to do with the Coven?"

"Why can't Rebecca Nurse's spirit just appear and make it easier?"

Amy glanced up from the family Bible where she was still going through all the pages. She shrugged, having no answer to offer.

John nodded, amazed yet again at how much he missed Rebecca Nurse, then went back to work, going through the last few books on the shelf but not finding any other marginal notations. He looked up, feeling a mounting sense of desperation as he realized just how much he had been counting on finding a new set of clues that could tell him something, anything about where to start looking for his daughter.

"We have nothing," he said, hearing the hollowness in his voice.

Amy shut the family Bible with a resounding thump. John noticed she looked much less defeated than he felt. Her eyes glittered with energy and spirit, and he felt a flush of admi- ration for her resilience. Today there was no vestige of the fear he knew she'd felt the night before in the underground passage, the same fear that he had felt deep in his bones then and that still troubled him today. As if Amy held the spirit of Rebecca Nurse, he wanted to reach out and extract her fire into his own belly because he had never felt so pathetically weak.

"Remember where you went with Rich Harvey?"

He blinked as her question interrupted his thoughts. "I went a lot of places with Rich."

"I'm talking about the Peabody Essex Institute. If I'm remembering correctly, you went to the Phillips Library there and met with somebody who let you see the old collections."

John rapped a knuckle on his forehead, as if trying to knock the dust off his brain. "I think his name was Joe D'Angelo. He's the head archivist." He felt his pulse quicken as he recalled the boxes of old journals and letters that were discovered recently in the House of the Seven Gables and donated to the museum. Even though the journal and letters hadn't been properly catalogued, D'Angelo had let him go through them with Rich when they visited the library. That was where he had found papers written by Nathaniel Hawthorne titled *The Truth about the Witch Trials of Salem,* papers that by careful design had been hidden away because Hawthorne feared the Coven's retaliation against his family. The same day John had read the Hawthorne document, Rich Harvey had claimed to be reading church documents written by pastors of nineteenth-century Salem congregations.

But what if Rich had lied about that, just as he had lied about so many other things? What if there had been something else buried in that box of old documents, the importance of which might only be clear to someone who knew the workings of the Coven. Someone like Rich. John knew he might be grasping at straws, but what if there had been something in those boxes of documents and letters that could shed light on Elizabeth Turner, on the reason Captain John Bancroft Andrews might have written "Ashtoreth/Astarte = Elizabeth Turner" in the margins of *Paradise Lost*?

Thinking again about those margin notes gave him a fresh flicker of hope, but as quickly as his spirits started to rise, they fell back to earth. "Even if we find something about Elizabeth Turner, what are the chances it has anything at all to do with Sarah?" He put his face in his hands. "The truth is it probably has a zero chance of helping us find Sarah, and I'm only doing it because I can't stand to sit around doing nothing."

Amy came over, took his by the shoulders, and gave him a gentle shake. "How will you know until you find it?"

CHAPTER ELEVEN

They finished searching the house without any further discoveries, and by then it was already early afternoon. John had put a call in to Joe D'Angelo but hadn't yet gotten a call back from the archivist, so he was left with nothing to do but pace and worry about Sarah.

He tried to sit down and make a checklist of places he thought they might have taken her, but after twenty minutes he ripped it up, knowing he was doing nothing but throwing darts in the dark. The truth was he had no idea where she was and no idea where to start looking.

He kept pacing the house, but every time he walked past the liquor cabinet it called out to him. He knew if he stayed in the house, he'd start drinking, and in terms of helping Sarah, which would be the worst possible thing he could do. Amy had already gone to the *Salem News* to help the other members of the paper's staff who had been working since early that morning to finalize their plans for renting furniture and computers and were hammering out the logistics of moving their offices on Friday so that they would be able to put out their first edition of *The Salem Observer* on Monday.

Left with nothing else to take the edge off his anxiety, he locked up the house and hurried over to the paper. He told no one about Sarah, apologized for his absence, and spent the rest of the afternoon pretending to concentrate as the people around him worked feverishly to finalize plans. At a staff meeting at the end of the day, the group decided that for the first week they would deliver the paper at no cost to all the *Salem News* subscribers. Once the subscriber base saw that the new paper was like the old one, everyone thought they would be likely to subscribe to *The Salem Observer*. John voted for the suggestion in agreement with the others, trying to feign an enthusiasm he didn't feel.

John was grateful at the way Amy and the other staffers seized the initiative because his mind was so much on Sarah that he could barely think about anything else. With all the arduous work and activity in the offices, he could see the fear in the eyes of everyone on the paper's staff. He knew all of them were frightened for their jobs and their economic well-being, and he struggled to appear focused and upbeat, knowing they looked to him to supply the newspaper's leadership. He gave his best effort to give them what they needed, he wanted to scream that he didn't really care about money or jobs or anything else when his daughter's life was on the line. It was everything he could do to bite his tongue and hold his raging anxiety inside.

At one point when the others were all busy, Jack Daniels sidled into John's office. "Everything okay?" he asked. "I wondered when you weren't around this morning."

"Yeah, yeah, I just had an appointment."

"Not getting cold feet on the new paper, are you?" "Absolutely not."

"You'd tell us if you weren't a hundred percent, right?" "Yes, and I'm very much a hundred percent."

Jack nodded. "I'll tell the others. People are just a little bit nervous; you understand."

"Completely." John hesitated as Jack started to turn and walk out of the office. "Jack," he said, causing Jack to stop and turn back. "I just need to tell you that I've got a bit of a personal problem. I can't seem to get hold of my daughter, and I'm a bit concerned. I don't mean to burden you with my problems, but it's got me a little distracted, that's all."

Jack stepped back into the office. "Your daughter's missing?" he asked in a deep voice.

John shrugged. "Maybe," he said, telling the version of the story he had concocted with Amy earlier that morning. "We're just not sure yet. It might be nothing, but she was supposed to have come over for dinner last night, and she never showed up."

"Have you contacted the police?"

"Not yet. I don't want to sound the alarm bells if it's not necessary." He checked his watch. "I need to call her office and see if anyone there has heard from her." "Jeez, John, that's terrible. Let me know if there's any-

thing any of us can do. And don't worry about getting things set up here; we've got everything well in hand. If you need to take time for yourself, just take it, okay?"

John nodded. "Thanks, but Jack... just keep it to your- self, okay?"

"Sure thing."

As Jack walked away, a cold feeling settled into John's stomach and he found himself wondering if Jack Daniels was just what he seemed on the surface, a person concerned about a friend and fellow worker, or if he was another secret member of the Salem Coven. John shook his head, hating that he could harbor that kind of suspicion about someone who'd never acted like anything but a friend, but at the same time admitting to himself he had no choice but to distrust the motives of everyone around him.

He said nothing else to the other staffers about the fact that Sarah was missing. However, as the afternoon wore on, he found himself studying each person, trying to detect any- thing unusual in their demeanor or in the way they looked at him or spoke to him. Even when he pretended to be reading something at his desk, he watched the others out of the corner of his eye, hoping to notice somebody staring at him when they thought he wasn't looking.

He wanted so badly for someone to give themselves away so that then he would have a person to pound on, a neck to wring, eyeballs to gouge until they gave him the information he wanted. He knew he was becoming a paranoid wreck, but he couldn't help it. He had to accept the probability that at least one member of his staff was also a member of the Coven. Even though he focused hard he saw nothing that made him suspicious.

Five minutes before seven o'clock, he closed the door of his office and called Sarah's television station and asked to speak with her boss, the producer. The person who answered took John's name and phone number and said that while the producer had gone home a bit earlier, he would try and reach the producer on his cell phone and give him the message. John's phone rang three minutes later.

John told the producer he was Sarah's father and had been worried since she didn't show up for a dinner the previous night. The producer hesitated then told John that Sarah had also not shown up for her morning news show, and that he, too, was concerned. "It's not at all like her to have an unexplained absence," the man said. "She is extremely conscientious."

"Yes," John agreed, "in everything."

"Have you called the police to report her missing, Mr.

Andrews?" the man asked.

"No," John replied. "Until now I kept hoping that might be premature. I kept thinking she might have had a personal reason for avoiding dinner, but she hasn't answered her cell phone or office phone all day."

"In our business it's extremely unusual for a news professional to miss a broadcast, especially when they don't call in first. If you want, we can call the police and file a missing person's report. That way, if it turns out Sarah's absence is something completely innocent, you won't be the one who gets blamed by your daughter for calling the cops."

"Yes, thank you very much, I'd really appreciate that."

John hung up, hoping he'd managed to deal with Sarah's abduction in a way that made it look normal. A second later he shook his head and let out a humorless laugh, wondering how far over the edge he'd gone when he could even think about an abduction as being "normal."

He glanced at his watch, wondered if he could still make a call to the Phillips Library at the Peabody Essex Institute before they closed, and he dialed the number. When someone answered, he asked for the second time to speak with Joe D'Angelo.

When D'Angelo came on the line John said, "I'm sorry to be a pest. I don't know if you remember me, but I came to the library a few weeks ago with Rich Harvey, and you were kind enough to let us look at the documents you'd just received from the House of the Seven Gables."

"Yes, I remember you," D'Angelo said. "I've been tied up in meetings all day and didn't have a chance until now to return phone calls. What a tragedy about Rich. I was absolutely devastated to hear it. I saw him often. I never would have guessed he was suicidal."

"I agree," John said, and then after a suitable pause, he continued, "I know Rich was working on several ideas for scholarly articles using those new documents as his sources.

I wanted to have the paper draft an article honoring Rich's scholarship and his contributions to helping us better under- stand our own local history. I was wondering if you might allow me to come back in and look over those same documents again?"

There was a pause while D'Angelo seemed to think it over. "Well, you're not an academic and those documents haven't even been catalogued yet. Usually, the only people allowed into our Rare Book and Manuscript Collection are working on academic projects, but in this case, I certainly believe we should make an exception. I think that article would be a wonderful idea."

Having made an appointment for early the next morning, John got off the phone with D'Angelo, and then made three more quick phone calls, first for a case of cold beer to be delivered from a nearby deli and then for pizza and takeout Chinese. Everything arrived around eight and everyone took a break and ate and drank a couple of beers. Afterward they continued to plan out the first edition of the new paper, worked on the masthead design, the typefaces, and other issues.

At about nine o'clock, John told the staff it was time to go home. They would meet tomorrow and continue the process. People wandered out to their cars, while he and Amy stayed behind to lock up and turn off the lights.

"Want some company?" Amy asked. "Or would you rather be alone?"

"Please come over," John said, rubbing his eyes and realizing how absolutely drained he was. That thought brought another reflection, that he was the most unromantic man on the face of the earth. How many other men, given the chance to sleep in the same bed with a woman who looked like Amy, would have done anything but hold her the nights they had been together? "I have nothing left, but I'd sure like to know you're there beside me."

She came up and placed her hands on his chest. "Life is going to get better, and then we're going to live like normal people."

He looked at her and nodded. "I hope so."

When they got back to his house, John went upstairs, took a shower, and got into bed, feeling so tired he expected to be asleep before his head hit the pillow.

As soon as he closed his eyes, he had the strange sensation he was someplace else, and his eyes snapped open. Only when he looked around, he realized he must have been dreaming because he felt just as exhausted and wrung out as he had before he got into bed.

He was on a narrow dirt road that wound along between two hilly pastures. A stone wall ran along the path on both sides of the road, and beyond the wall's sheep grazed the hill- side. He was alone, and even though he had the feeling he'd been to this place before, he didn't recognize it at first.

Ahead of him the road curved sharply and ran beneath the branches of a huge and ancient tree. The shade beneath the tree seemed unnaturally dark, and when he focused on it, he remembered the girl he had seen walking down this same road. He had been afraid for the girl because she had been walking toward a place where he had sensed the presence of great evil. Now, even though he sensed all those things again, when he tried to stop walking, he found he couldn't. His feet just kept moving as if someone else was controlling them and forcing him to take step after step.

Up ahead the darkness got closer and closer, and it was moving rather than him, and then a second later he was inside it and following the road around a sharp bend to where he could see a house in the distance. The feeling of incipient danger grew even stronger. The house was old and austere but nothing unusual, just a clapboard structure like many in

New England, with a steep pitched roof and a number of chimneys and gabled windows along the top.

Something about the house made him want to stay faraway. His feelings of dread were growing stronger by the second, but they weren't powerful enough to overcome whatever force was drawing him onward. He came to the outside of the house and finally managed to bring himself to a halt. There was no one else in sight, but he was certain the house was not empty. A feeling of great evil radiated from its walls like heat pulsing from an oven.

He looked at the downstairs windows, but at first, he could see nothing because the light reflected off the glass and made them opaque. After another second he caught a flicker of motion in one of the upstairs windows, and when he tilted his head upward, he recognized Sarah. She was standing very straight, her hands behind her back as if they might have been bound. Sarah was looking down at him, but her lips weren't moving. She was not trying to call out to him, she was staring at him, and her eyes seemed cold and distant.

Upon seeing her, John ran to the front door and tried to open it, but it wouldn't budge. He kicked it and then slammed his shoulder into the wood, but it was thick and well-built and would not budge. He went around to the windows and tried to raise them, and when that didn't work, he tried to break one by throwing a rock through it, but the rock just bounced off the glass. It was like a force field was protecting the entire house.

It didn't hurt him physically to touch the force field, but each time he met it he saw terrible, familiar images that stung him as if they were electric shocks. His mind conjured pictures of dead bodies, horribly mangled and disfigured, and walls smeared with blood. He smelled the overpowering copper stench from vast quantities of spilled blood and the reek of feces from disemboweled and ruptured intestines.

Almost brought to his knees by the images, he jerked away from the wall, but even as he did, he realized the pictures in his head weren't of the underground room where the Salem Coven had performed their horrible blood sacrifices. The room looked similar but was different somehow. He suddenly felt a terrible chill as he realized that the pictures were telling him that Salem wasn't the only place, that there were other killing rooms equally as horrible as the tile-walled room beneath Salem.

He backed away farther and looked up at the window again, but now Sarah was gone. In her place he saw the young girl he had seen walking the dirt road during his dream nights earlier. She was looking down at him, her skin the pallor of death, her mouth running bloody on both sides, her eyes dead.

He woke up wide-eyed and sweating and breathing like a bellows. Beside him Amy slept soundly. He knew she must have been just as exhausted as he felt because he had not managed to wake her. He sat with his skin drying in the cool air as he stared through the half-open curtains at the dark harbor and the darker ocean beyond.

He knew without any doubt that something was happening to him that he could not explain. Whatever it was, it wasn't like it had been when he'd seen the spirit of Rebecca Nurse. That had been strange and disorienting at first, but at least it had been outside his body. What he felt now was that a door was opening somewhere in his mind, and in some way, it was connecting him to things that were far away, but which were also real, or were at least close to real.

The only thing that made him believe these dream/visions were not the beginning of madness was that he was certain in a strange, yet inexplicable way they were connected to Sarah. Somehow, if he could learn to interpret them and understand them, it would help him get his daughter back. At least that's what he wanted to believe.

CHAPTER TWELVE

The next morning John pulled into the parking lot at the Peabody Essex Institute at eight o'clock sharp, climbed out of the car and dragged his exhausted body toward Plummer Hall. More than anything he would have loved to have stayed in bed because he felt as if he'd barely slept. He'd finally managed to fall back to sleep again the night before, but only after lying awake exhausted and unable to calm down after the dream that had awakened him. The Phillips Library usually opened at nine, but Joe D'Angelo had a busy day, and so he had asked John to come before the regular operating hours. True to his word, D'Angelo was standing outside the front doors as John arrived.

"Thank you for doing this," John said.

"Not a problem," said D'Angelo, shivering slightly as he turned, opened the door, and ushered John inside. He was tall and thin with bony shoulder bones that stuck up like two knobs beneath his threadbare cardigan sweater. His mostly bald scalp was unusually pink, from the cold John thought, and D'Angelo's glasses were fogged up from having come out of the warm library into the morning chill.

"I hope you weren't waiting for me for long," John said, glancing at his watch to make sure he wasn't late.

D'Angelo shook his head. "It wasn't being outside. It's being inside with the overheated library, and then going into the freezing rare books section and then back into the over-heated library. I'm either too hot or freezing all day long. It's no wonder I have a perpetual cold."

D'Angelo walked him through the main reading room, then opened a door that said "Private" and led the way down a flight of steps to another door marked "Rare Books and Manuscripts Section. Restricted Access." He opened the door's electronic lock with a magnetic card that hung around his neck. John followed the archivist into a small room where there were coat hangers for extraneous clothing and cubby- holes for personal effects. There were also five or six navy blue cardigan sweaters hanging together at one end of the coat rack with "Property of Phillips Library" stenciled in white letters along the back. On the far wall was another door that read:

NO FLASH PHOTOGRAPHY

WEAR GLOVES AT ALL TIMES

NO FOOD OR DRINK ALLOWED

John had been here once before and knew the drill. He took off his overcoat, hung it up, donned one of the cardigan sweaters, and then went over to the transparent plastic box that hung from the wall and took a pair of white cloth gloves. While John put on the gloves, D'Angelo reached into the pocket of his cardigan, pulled out his own pair of gloves, and put them on. Then he opened the next door and led the way into the rare books room. Right away, John felt the temperature and humidity change. The room was cooler than the rest of the library. When he looked at the instruments on the wall, he saw that the temperature in the room was sixty- five degrees, and the humidity was 45 percent.

"You want to see the same material you were looking at the last time?" D'Angelo asked.

John nodded, and the archivist disappeared into the stacks and came out a minute later with three boxes that he placed on one of the research tables. John opened the first box and felt his pulse quicken as he saw the stacks of letters and other writings all carefully organized and separated. D'Angelo cleared his throat before John did anything else, and when John looked up the archivist reviewed with him the proper methods for separating and overseeing the ancient pages to avoid any possibility of damage.

John sat down at the table and began to carefully remove the documents from the first box and look through them. There were letters from various early residents of Salem, personal journals from people whose names meant nothing. He saw pages of farm reports, recording the corn, wheat, and sorghum one of the Putnam farms had produced, how many oxen, cows, pigs and sheep they owned. He saw the document written by Nathaniel Hawthorne and skipped past it because he'd already read it.

John went through the first box and the second without finding anything that gave him pause. He was on the con- tents of the third box, close to the bottom, his eyes starting to glaze over when he found a packet of three letters bound together with a navy-blue ribbon. He gently slipped the rib- bon off the letters, unfolded them, and began to look them over.

At once he saw that the letter was addressed, "Dear Elizabeth." He felt his pulse kick because it was the first thing, he'd seen that related to the curious notation in *Paradise Lost*.

He struggled to read the old-fashioned writing and he thought it said, "Thee hast been well pre- pared for thy role and responsibilities. Be thee obedient to thy

Expert and diligent in thy duties and remember fondly those who hath trained thee for thy Greatness in the New World. We hope this letter finds thee well in that far place and that the Astarte brought thee safely to the shores of your new home in reasonable comfort and without undue travail." The Astarte! It must have been a ship, John realized. But then what did *Ashtoreth/Astarte = Elizabeth Turner* mean? How did a person equate to a ship? If Astarte was the name of the ship that had brought Elizabeth Turner to North America, why was that important enough to call for a margin note in his great-great-grandfather's book?

He looked through the other papers, which had been sinched together by the same ribbon, but were addressed to different people, within the same family, but shed no further light on his questions. The only other piece of paper in the packet was curious because it consisted of two renderings, the first of a house with lines drawn through it, and the second on the bottom half of the page showed a world map with lines radiating outward from what looked like the southwest corner of England.

Something about the drawings caught his eye, and he stared at them for a time trying to understand their meaning. Whatever their purpose, they were meticulous. The drawing of the house, which resembled the wealthier homes in Salem, was a house with six gables, each of the gables being the beginning of one of the lines. The house was oriented specifically to lines of the compass, with north, south, east, and west shown separate from the lines that radiated from the gables. Below it, the larger map was carefully executed, and its purpose seemed to be to extend the lines from the gables out- ward around the world.

John looked at where the lines intersected with land and noted that one of those points seemed to cut through the northern coast of North America, close to where the colony of Massachusetts was found. Another line went through Northern Europe and Russia. The lines were confusing because they didn't seem to have any real meaning that John could figure out. Also, because the house from which the lines originated was irregular in its design, the lines did not radiate evenly. They weren't anything like the spokes of a wheel but shot off at odd angles. Thus, another line went through Southern China and crossed what John guessed would be North Korea. Another went through Central Africa, another bisected South America and Mexico.

Why had someone gone to such trouble and put such effort into a paper drawing? John wondered. Were these supposed to be trade routes? He didn't think that made any sense, but then what was the purpose? He was sure that Puritans hadn't believed in wasting time on non- essential tasks, and yet a lot of artistry and time had been spent to make the drawings. Another question was, if they were so important, why hadn't the artist made it larger and put it on canvas instead of paper? Then, other questions occurred to him. To whom had this been sent? There was no other writing on the page, no sign of the recipient.

He looked at the folds in the paper then laid out the other letters that had been in the bundle. Wondering if the map had was folded along with one of the other letters, he took the pages one by one and laid them atop the map. The creases on only one of the letters exactly matched the map's folds, as if the same careful hand had folded them at the same time. It was the letter written to someone known only as Elizabeth.

John felt a surge of fresh energy as he looked at the letter and the map. The references to greatness and obedience to a master, to a ship named *Astarte*, and now the lines that radiated off the gables of the house, one of which intersected the Americas at what looked like the location of modern-day Salem. All of it was vague, but he knew he was onto something here, something strange. He didn't have any idea what it meant yet or where it might lead, but he knew in his gut he had to start pulling this thread to see where it led, and he had to do it as fast as he could. He couldn't articulate why, but he believed that wherever this went, it was going to take him to Sarah.

He knew it was against library policy, but he snuck his cell phone out of his pocket and used it to take pictures of both documents. Then he returned the documents to the box and rang the buzzer that would summon Joe D'Angelo to come let him out and return their boxes to their proper places.

CHAPTER THIRTEEN

John was back in his car by half past nine but sat in the parking lot, the engine turned off, and drummed his fingers on the steering wheel. He didn't know where to go or what to do. He'd learned a little bit more about the Coven, at least *maybe* he had, but how was it going to help him find Sarah?

He needed to do something, but there was nothing he *could* do. He had no information, no course of action. In addition, he knew he needed to at least show his face at the *Salem News* and pretend to work. However, instead of heading straight to the paper, he drove back to his house. Needing to take a run to try to banish his exhaustion and wear down the anxiety that was going to make him useless if he couldn't get it under control quickly, he changed into his running clothes, did a cursory stretch, and then headed out. As he began to jog, he tried to empty his mind of conscious thoughts about Sarah or Elizabeth Turner or *Astarte*, and instead let his inquiries and associations run free and seek order on their own.

The drawing of the house and the lines coming off the gables and extending around the world had disturbed him for reasons he couldn't articulate. It was stuck in his mind, because when he closed his eyes, he could still see it as if it had been burned into his retina. Who exactly was Elizabeth Turner? What part of England had she come from? Who had her master been? What was the significance of the name of the ship on which she had sailed to the New World? Was it just coincidence that she ship's name, *Astarte*, was also the name of one of the angels who had helped Luci- fer in his rebellion against God in *Paradise Lost*? And even so, what could any of this have to do with Sarah?

Why did he have such a strong compulsion to dig into history when his daughter was missing in the present? Was it because he just needed to do something to feel like he was making progress, or were his instincts guiding him in the right direction? And what about the dream or the vision he'd had on two different nights of the girl walking on a dirt lane and a house that looked exactly as though it could be the one in the drawing? And what about seeing Sarah in the window of that house? What did it mean?

He remembered the idea he'd discussed with Amy before Sarah was abducted, going to England to try and find Jessica Lodge, and then he began to wonder whether his dream was somehow related to Sarah's current location? Was it possible she was spirited out of the country? Certainly, if his suspicions about Jessica Lodge were correct and if Jessica was the rumored Inquisitor of the Salem Coven, then she might have had Sarah abducted and flown to England, to someplace where the Coven still operated in secrecy. Jessica certainly had the financial means to have pulled it off; she had her own jet.

He made a mental note to check with the FAA to see if Jessica Lodge's jet had flown back into the US at any time in the past few days and if it had left again, and if it had, where its flight plan said it was heading.

He let his eyes wander along with his thoughts as he ran through the streets of Salem, past the familiar, ancient houses, so many of which dated back to the 1700s. The town, which so often seemed overly full of tourists, especially during the two months preceding Halloween, now appeared blessedly empty, since Halloween had just been a week earlier. He passed Wicca Wonders, the occult shop run by Abigail Putnam, the woman who had been the head of Salem Coven and who had reported to the rumored Inquisitor.

At this point it seemed so impossible that it was like recalling a strange dream to think back to the night he killed Abigail along with the other leaders of the Coven. He still couldn't begin to explain exactly what triggered it when an extreme combination of anger and fear and God only knew what else had allowed him to absorb the spirit of Rebecca Nurse and the spirit of a young woman named Melissa Blake. Also, attached to Melissa Black had been a chain of other spirits, all of whom had been sacrificed by the Coven, and the joint force of all those spirits had joined with his own and coalesced into occult power. And he had used that power to destroy those Coven leaders.

Once the killing was over, the power had rushed out of his body as quickly as it had come. It left him dazed and utterly exhausted and, just like right now, wondering whether any of what he thought had just happened had really happened. Only the ravaged and torn bodies of the dead Coven leaders convinced him that it had been real.

John closed his eyes and picked up his speed as recalled how he had taken Captain Card down into the Coven's cata- combs to show him the bodies, at the time never suspecting that Card was also an imposter, who himself must have been part of the Coven. Only if Card was a member of the Coven, why had he told John there was one more member of the Coven who had not been in the catacombs that night? Card had called that person the Inquisitor, the most powerful member, one who made sure the other members of the Coven remained true to their sworn purpose.

What motive could a member of the Coven have for leading him deeper to the truth? He had wondered more than once if it was even true, but in his guts, he had the sense it was. Did the Coven want him to go to England to look for Jessica Lodge? Was there something about Salem itself, the fact John's ancestors were buried here, and their physical proximity was what had allowed him to tap into that extraordinary spiritual power? The Coven realized that in England, so far from those ancestral graves, he would be powerless and easy to kill.

He shook his head in confusion and picked up his pace even more. He could feel his heart beating hard, his lungs bellowing in and out, his legs pumping, burning out at least for the moment, the effects of his exhaustion. There simply *had* to have been a purpose behind Card's revelation, he told himself, and he needed to figure out what it was. Also, after Card had taken such pains to mislead him into thinking he was a police officer, why had Card suddenly stopped returning John's phone calls and thereby abandoned his carefully crafted charade? It would have been so easy to have kept John in the dark. What was the point in letting him learn he'd been duped?

Was there something about restarting the paper that could have triggered Card's dis-appearance? Was restarting the paper the thing that had triggered Sarah's abduction? He turned a corner and ran hard down another long familiar street. He saw the houses and businesses and restaurants without really seeing anything. He could feel his brain cork-screwing into questions, getting further and further into a web of confusion where there were absolutely no answers. He wanted to stop, pull out his hair, and scream.

But then he did stop. Dead. Right in the middle of the street, and a car behind him honked its horn and swerved. John ignored the horn and stared straight ahead at the thing that had caused him to make such an abrupt halt.

It was a sign for the entrance into the compound where the House of the Seven Gables was found. He couldn't see the house from here, but its shape was in his mind. How many times had he seen it looming dark and austere and spooky because of its sharp angles and the steep gables for which it was named? As he stared at the sign, his mind started to race in a new direction, and he began making connections.

The House of the Seven Gables wasn't the house from his dreams, and it wasn't the house in the drawing he'd found that morning in the library, but it was so similar. Just like the other historic houses and building in Salem, he'd seen the House of the Seven Gables so many times over so many years that he had taken it for granted, but now in his mind he was seeing it, really seeing it for the first time in a long time. He remembered the journal he had found on an earlier visit to the Phillips Library when he had gone with Rich Har- vey. Written by his ancestor, Captain John Bancroft Andrews, the journal had talked about Captain Andrews's friendship with Nathaniel Hawthorne. This in turn reminded John of another connection that hadn't seemed vitally important. Hawthorne's cousin had built the House of the Seven Gables, and that cousin's name had been Captain John Turner, the same man who, John surmised, had married a woman named Elizabeth Turner, as in Ashtoreth/Astarte = Elizabeth Turner. Was it the same Elizabeth Turner as the woman in the letters? What were the odds in a small community like Salem there could have been two Elizabeth Turners?

Earlier that day he'd skipped past his great-great-grand- father's journal because he'd read it on the other occasion he'd visited the library, but now he was thinking those boxes of recently discovered papers he had gone through just that morning at the Phillips had included some of Hawthorne's secret writing done at the end of his life. Hawthorne had wanted those truths shared, but he had also intended those writings discovered only after his death when his family could no longer be harmed as an act of vengeance.

And hadn't those recently found boxes of old letters and journals been taken from the House of the Seven Gables? The house was a tourist magnet, John thought. Where in that structure, which had been crawled through by so many hundreds of thousands of visitors, could those documents have been hidden for all those years? And if those letters and journals had just been discovered, what else remained? And hadn't Hawthorne, just like Andrews, been descended from some of the people who had been part of the original Salem Coven.

Hawthorne's family name had originally been Hathorne. John Hathorne had been one of the original judges in the witchcraft trials and one of the original Salem Coven mem- bers. Deeply shamed by his ancestor's involvement in those despicable trials, Nathaniel Hawthorne had changed his name to disguise his relationship. John Andrews's own family bore the same stain because on his mother's side he was descended from the

Putnam's. Edward Putnam had was implicated in the witchcraft trials and a member of the original Salem Coven, and yet another of his ancestors, Ann Putnam, had been one of Rebecca Nurse's original accusers. John suspected that one of the reasons Rebecca Nurse had picked him and chosen to appear to him was that he bore the blood of the Putnam's in his veins, in addition to the blood of Captain John Bancroft Andrews. John found the whole line of inquiry uncomfortable, but he could not help but wonder whether his Putnam blood was what had made it possible for him to open the secret doors that led to the Coven's lair beneath the streets and cemeteries of Salem. Did his Putnam blood also carry a deeper stain, one that in the wrong circumstances might make him susceptible to the Coven's dark call? Did he share that trait in a dark hidden recess of his being? He had wondered about that over the past two weeks, but each time the question arose he'd tried to shove it down into the back of his mind, as if keeping it unasked would mean it couldn't be true.

As John continued to stare at the entrance to the House of the Seven Gables compound, he could feel the force pulling at him that seemed as powerful and impossible to resist as gravity. He *needed* to go into the compound. He *needed* to see the house up close, even go inside, but he had no idea what he hoped to carry out if he did. The House of the Seven Gables was a tourist mecca. There was public access to most parts of the house, and there were sections that were closed off. The parts that were closed to the public, would have been searched throughout the years. The question surfaced again, where would those recently discovered documents have come from? Giving into his growing compulsion, he walked across the street and headed into the compound. The sign said that the House of the Seven Gables opened at ten a.m. for tours, and when he checked his watch, he saw that it was seven minutes past and that two busses had already pulled in, one full of school children and the other full of retirees. Both busses were in the parking lot disgorging their passengers. The children whooped and tried to run around while teachers tried to corral them. The old people moved much more slowly.

John went into the front building, bought a ticket for a guided tour, and watched as the teachers' bought tickets for the kids and the bus driver bought tickets for the retirees. He waited around, trying to mask his impatience, until a tour guide finally came out and addressed the group. The tour guide apologized for the extra-large group on the day's first tour, saying that two of the other guides who were usually there had both called in sick.

After a quick history lesson, the guide cautioned the group not to touch anything in the house or go beyond the ropes the tour set out. The school children jostled and shoved their way into the lead, while the retirees strung out behind. John went last, trailing the stragglers of the older group and found him- self far behind the tour guide from the very beginning.

Ahead of him the slowest of the oldsters hobbled on walkers and moved like snails through the door of the House of the Seven Gables, and as they did John let himself drop even farther behind. His eyes carefully roamed each room as he walked inside the house, seeing the period furnishings, the low ceilings, the large fireplaces, the floors grooved from hundreds of years of foot traffic. He took in all of it, but looked hard for other, less obvious things.

He lagged behind rest of the tour through the first floor, he saw nothing of interest. There were two sitting rooms, a dining room, and a good-sized kitchen with a large hearth with iron kettles on iron hangers and a bread oven built into the side.

On the far side of the kitchen, a decorative rope barrier stood in front of a small door set into the wall. John waited for a time, but a group of five or six of the retirees remained in the kitchen, fascinated by the cooking utensils and the baking oven.

He finally moved out of the kitchen and caught another group of retirees as they were heading up the stairs to the second floor. They went up slowly and milled around, going through the rooms. John had the same sense of disappointment when he got up there as he'd had on the first floor, and he went through the bedrooms quickly, seeing nothing of interest.

By the time he came back downstairs, the school kids were all back in the dining room where the tour guide was showing them the famous hidden staircase, made immortal in Nathaniel Hawthorne's novel, *The House of the Seven Gables.* The kids were taking turns going up and coming back down in groups of five, and the retirees were showing the same interest in the secret staircase as the children.

Slowly, the rest of the stragglers made their way into the dining room as people went up the secret staircase that wound around the chimney to a small room in the attic and then came back down. Realizing this was his only chance, John moved out of the dining room and back into the kitchen, glanced over his shoulder to make sure no one else had come after him, and then he went over to the guard rope and tried the latch on the door that stood behind it.

To his delight, the latch clicked softly, and the door opened. John ducked under the rope, went quickly through the door, and quietly shut it behind. Finding himself in complete darkness, he reached into his pocket for his cell phone, went to the flashlight app, and flicked it on. He played the light around and saw that he was standing on a narrow landing and a steep set of stairs led down to what looked like a large cellar.

The air here was musty and damp, smelling of great age and mildew. The steps were as steep as the rungs of a ladder, and John descended carefully, keeping one hand against the side of the wall for balance. At the bottom he shined his small light into the darkness, seeing that the space was low, cavernous, and empty, broken only by brick columns that no doubt helped bear the weight of the beams above and the huge brick-supports that helped bear the weight of the fire- places and chimneys overhead.

Above his head John could hear the footsteps clomping around on the wooden floor-boards, and he realized the tour was starting to go outside the house. Wishing he had a candle or larger flashlight, he started moving around the cellar, trying to see whether there could be anything here that might shed more light on all his questions. For some reason, the sensation he'd first experienced outside, the feeling as if something were pulling him into the house, had become even stronger since he'd come into the cellar.

Shining the light on the dirt floor, John could see where the dirt was worn out in a line, as if over the years many people had come in the same direction across the cellar floor and made a flat area in the otherwise lumpy dirt. The dirt path went from the bottom of the steps toward the far end of the cellar, and not having any better idea, John started to follow it to where it ended in a massive brick support for the line of fireplaces and chimneys that ran up the far side of the house.

He stopped at the brick support and shined his light around. The cell phone was becoming hot to the touch, and he knew he couldn't keep the light on too much longer. He looked up and down the support, but he could see no reason for the path to end right here. The phone got hotter and hotter in his hand, and he was about to give up and head back when something occurred to him.

He patted his pockets, but because he was dressed in his running clothes and not street clothes, he did not have his pocketknife in his pocket as he usually would. Casting his eyes around the brick support one more time, he looked for another instrument he could use, and after a second his gaze fastened on something that glinted, reflecting the light from his beam. He reached for the thing, and his fingers closed around a thin nail that was resting on a line of bricks. He took the nail, and without giving any more than a momentary thought to the risk of tetanus, he jabbed the tip of the nail into the first finger of his left hand.

Immediately a thick dot of blood welled to the surface, and then he looked around for the right place to put it. Spot- ting a place where the bricks appeared cleaner, as if people had inadvertently wiped up against them and cleaned off the dust of centuries that clung to the other bricks, he ran his other hand up along the higher rows of bricks until he felt it, something smooth and cool like a very shallow and very small bowl.

Placing the first finger of his left hand into the indentation, he felt the surface soften instantly, as if the metal or whatever he was touching had become porous and his blood was being sucked in. A second later he heard a *thud* and the heavy object had shifted, and then part of the brick support swung outward as if on perfectly smooth hinges to reveal another staircase.

The cell phone was nearly burning the fingers of his right hand now, but he ignored the pain and started climbing, taking care to be as silent as possible. Just like the other secret staircase, this one was very narrow and very steep, running around what must have been the fireplace chimney on the far end of the house. John went up and up, high enough that he knew he had to be coming up to the third floor of the house, and he finally spotted a narrow landing with a door- way ahead of him.

As he came to the doorway, he noticed something else, a heavy and terrible smell, of a dead animal, trapped in the wall. He listened, his mind fighting against the image that was trying to form, trying to reject the possibility that the smell could be coming from something that had once been human. Finally, with a trembling hand he lifted the latch and pulled the door open. Light flooded into the area where he was standing.

The smell really hit him. It was horrible, so disgusting and powerful it nearly drove him to his knees. He breathed through his mouth and swallowed hard until he was confident, he wouldn't vomit. The stench was so overwhelming his mind tried to grasp how it was possible that he hadn't smelled it before now? How could the rest of the house not reek? The question left his mind as quickly as it had come because in the next second his eyes focused on the interior of the room, and he saw the chair and the body tied to it.

His mind seized because his first thought was that it had to be Sarah and he nearly let out a blood-curdling scream. He leaned against the wall and took gulps of air and after a second he managed to get a modicum of self-control. After another second the small corner of his brain that was still capable of rational thought told him that this dead person could not have been Sarah because it was a man.

What came next was a feeling of almost insane relief. John felt a sense of hilarity he recognized as both pathetic and dangerous, but he couldn't help wanting to dance a jig to celebrate that someone else had died and not his daughter. He shook his head to try and dislodge those thoughts. As he crept forward, he tried to get a better look at the dead body in the chair.

At first, he noticed the skin, which was paste white with a greenish tinge. It looked like the person had been dead for days. Whoever they were, they had died a horrible death because he could see their fingers snipped off at the second knuckle. Was it done to prevent fingerprint identification, or to inflict pain? He assumed it must have been pain because he looked down and saw that the man's toes were cut in an equivalent manner. From the bruises and deep contusions, it looked like the bones of the feet had struck with a hammer.

The dead man's head sagged forward at an angle that made it impossible to see his face, but when John squatted to take a closer look, he grew squeamish. The man's nose was cut out, his eyes gouged, and his lips cut away.

Worst of all even with the massive damage, John recognized the face, and a chill went down his spine. The dead man in the chair was the person he had known as Captain Andrew Card.

CHAPTER FOURTEEN

J ohn reeled back, his mind empty of everything but shock until he felt his heel go over the edge and he nearly fell down the steep staircase. He quickly reached out and grabbed the doorframe to steady himself. Then he bent over and tried to slow his pounding heart before he stepped back into the room with the body.

When he looked at Andrew Card a second time, he saw the ropes that held his legs to the chair and the way his arms had been tied at the elbows and were pulled behind his back. John realized that whoever had done this had not wanted Card to die quickly, and the gruesome sight took him back to the night in the underground chamber when he'd found the two young people savagely eviscerated, their entrails spilling down across their legs.

John shuddered again, telling himself that Cabby Corwin was dead. John knew it because he was the one who'd killed him. If it hadn't been Cabby, who had done this? And why?

John had been so certain Andrew Card had been part of the Coven, especially when it turned out that he'd lied about being on the police force. Had the Coven turned on one of its own? If this was the case, what had Card done to incur their wrath?

Why had they left him here? This was clearly a room used by the Coven to torture, but the House of the Seven Gables *was* a major tourist attraction. Wouldn't someone notice the stench of a rotting body? But if that was true, why hadn't they noticed already? John could feel the wind coming up the staircase from the cellar, rising like smoke in a chimney, and he thought a natural draft took the air outside through a vent.

He thought for a moment about going through Card's pockets to see what he might find, but he couldn't bring himself to do it. Card's skin was already a horrible shade of green, and it looked like it was starting to slough off his body. Besides, John guessed that whoever had committed such a savage murder must have taken care to empty Card's pockets. After another moment of indecision, he backed out of the room, pushed the door closed, turned his cell phone flash- light app back on, and made his way quickly down to the cellar where he closed the hidden door in the bricks. Making his way back across the cellar, he climbed the steps to the kitchen and then paused to listen for sounds that would show a second tour group was someplace nearby.

Satisfied he was alone, he stepped out the door, pulled it closed, ducked beneath the velvet rope, and hurried out through the kitchen and the rest of the house. He came out the front door of the house just seconds ahead of the second tour group of the day. The person leading the tour recognized him from the first tour and looked at him in shock.

Trying to gather his wits and pretend he hadn't just seen something that scared him half to death, John did his best to look embarrassed and gave a half-hearted wave. "Sorry," he said, struggling to produce an excuse. "I just got so caught up in the atmosphere I had to go up that secret staircase a second time. I didn't realize everyone else had left already."

The tour guide scowled like a teacher who knew the student's dog hadn't really eaten the homework, but he had a group of people eager to see the house, so he just nodded. John hurried past the tour group and started back toward the street, walking across the gravel parking lot.

The school bus and the tour bus from earlier had already left, and the lot was deserted, except for where a couple was getting out of a car. They appeared to be tourists and they hurried toward him as they headed to the visitors' building to buy tickets. John paid them no attention because his brain was still reeling with shock. As the couple came abreast, the man stepped closer to John than necessary given all the space in the parking lot, but still John paid no attention until kidney punch sent a staggering shot of pain rocketing through his body.

In the next instant an arm came around his throat and began to squeeze. It had all happened so fast John could barely understand what was happening. He fought to get a breath but the arm around his throat was strong and squeezing off his airway. Out of the corner of his eye he could see the woman reach into her purse for something, and when her hand came free, John saw a hypodermic syringe. She stepped forward and brought the tip of the needle toward his neck.

John arched his back and tried to break out of the man's hold, but his attacker was too strong. He hooked his foot behind one of the man's legs and tried to trip him, but the man backed into a car and bent John backward, nearly lifting him off his feet.

John kicked at the woman, catching her full in the chest and knocking her back a step or two. Her face tightened in a grimace of pain, but she circled him again, this time from the side, jabbing the needle like the tip of a bayonet toward his exposed throat. John tried to kick again, but the man behind him swung him around so he was facing the hood of a car. There was absolutely nothing John could do.

He braced for the bite of the needle, but it never came. Instead, he heard two quick spitting sounds from someplace behind him, and then a half second later two more. The arm around his neck relaxed suddenly, and John nearly toppled backwards as the man's suddenly limp weight dragged against him and the man fell to the ground.

John held his throat and sucked air into his lungs as his brain tried to grasp what had just happened. Already hocked and totally disoriented, nothing prepared him for what he saw when he straightened up and turned around.

The man walking toward him as he unscrewed a long silencer from the tip of his pistol wore a broad-brimmed black fedora and a dark suit and black shirt that was topped with a Roman collar.

CHAPTER FIFTEEN

John blinked at the stranger, half in fear and half in astonishment. "Who are you? He stammered. "And what the hell is going on?"

The man tucked his pistol into a small shoulder holster. "Questions later," he said in an impossibly calm voice with a heavy European accent. "Help now."

The priest or whatever he was, grasped the dead man under his armpits and nodded toward his ankles. After a beat, John understood, and he bent over, grabbed the man's ankles, and helped carry the body back to the car the man and woman had just climbed out of. It was Ford Taurus and was unlocked. The priest opened the driver's side door and popped the trunk.

They put the body inside the trunk and went back for the woman. As they did, another car pulled into the lot and started past them. The priest stepped in front of the woman's body and squatted down, blocking her from view. The car went past, parked, and the people climbed out and went toward the visitor's building. As they disappeared, the priest stood, picked the woman up, and nodded for John to take her ankles.

Moving quickly, they carried her across to the Taurus and put her body into the trunk with the other one. John could see the two small holes in her temple and thin line of blood running from each one. There were two similar holes in the side of the man's head. He was still way too keyed up to think clearly, but the details told him the priest must have used a small caliber weapon because the bullets hadn't gone all the way through the skull and there was so little blood. The tight grouping of the shots on both bodies told him this man had to be a professional assassin, not a priest.

"Touch nothing," the priest said as he ran his hands up and down the two dead bodies, pulling car keys and a wallet from the pocket of the dead man and a pistol from a small holster in the man's belt and taking the woman's purse. He handed John the pistol without turning to look at him, and as he did John noted that the priest was wearing a pair of thin, black leather gloves, as if he had come prepared for violence, totally prepared not to leave fingerprints.

"You're not a priest, are you?" John demanded. "Questions later."

The priest finished searching the bodies, then closed the trunk. He fished into his own pocket and pulled out a second set of car keys. "You drive this one," he said, hitting a button that caused the taillights in a nearby Honda Civic to flash. "Follow."

The priest handed John the keys then climbed behind the wheel of the Taurus and started the engine. John hesitated a second then walked to the Honda, backed out, and followed the Taurus, not knowing what else he should do.

His head whirled with the craziness of what he had experienced in the past fifteen minutes. The fact that nobody appeared to have seen what had just happened, either to John or to his two attackers had to be a miracle, he thought, but then he remembered how the priest had acted when the car drove into the parking lot. The priest had been so cool headed, so totally calm as he squatted down and blocked the body from view.

They drove for slightly over thirty minutes, taking Route 107 South down toward Boston but then following the signs for Logan Airport. As they got close to the airport, they followed the signs toward long-term parking. John began to understand what the priest was doing. Then his mind began to race all over again as he wondered what the priest was going to want him to do after they had left the Taurus in long-term parking. Where had he come from? What had he been doing in the parking lot at the same time his attackers showed up? How could a priest carry a freaking gun and shoot two people? Was the man sane? Was he going to shoot John once he got done hiding the other two bodies.

All the questions that occurred, he just kept following the Taurus, reasoning that since the priest had just saved his life, he needed to assume the man didn't intend to do him any harm. Hadn't he just handed John the dead man's gun? John knew he had to assume the man was there to help him, but as to the man's reasons or identity, he had nothing but questions.

Ahead of him the Taurus turned into long-term parking and the priest stopped and got a ticket. John did the same, following the priest to the far back end of the lot. The priest found a parking spot he liked, backed the Taurus in, and climbed out. He checked the car carefully for any- thing he might have missed, then kept his head turned down so that it hid both his face and his collar from any security cameras in the area as he walked over and climbed into the passenger side of the Honda.

"Drive, please, and exit, then drive back to Salem." "We're just leaving the bodies here. We're not calling the police?"

"If you called them, what would you tell them, exactly?" The man threw John a sideways glance. "What did you tell them the last time?"

CHAPTER SIXTEEN

J ohn's throat was dry. "What last time?" he croaked, but he knew what the man was talking about.

"When you killed the Coven leaders. What would you have told the police?"

"I told Captain Card...who wasn't—"

"No, he wasn't a policeman, but he kept you from sounding like a madman or perhaps a psychopath."

"But the bodies weren't even there when I took him down the—how the hell do you know about that?"

The man ignored the question and pointed to the turn- off for Route 107 North toward Salem. John got onto 107 and waited until they were at cruising speed, safely tucked into the right lane, then he turned his head. "Okay, enough bullshit. Who are you?"

The priest looked at him, his bright blue eyes calm and guileless. "Father Rupert Faust."

Turning his eyes back to the road, John shook his head. "No way. Priests don't kill people."

"Not usually," Father Faust agreed, "but are people usually attacked in the parking lot of the House of the Seven Gables?"

"Of course not," John said, realizing the priest had just answered a question with another question. "Did you also know about the dead body on the third floor of the house?" Father Faust was silent for a moment. Then he said, "Yes, "in a hard voice.

"Did you kill him?" "Of course not."

John nodded. "Why was he killed?" he asked. "Do you know?"

"Two reasons," Faust said.

John waited for the priest to say more, and after a moment he let out a sigh. "What were they?"

"First, because the people who did it hated the man and what he stood for."

"What was that?"

"He fought the Coven."

John gripped the wheel hard, unable to hide his surprise. "You're saying Andrew Card was a good guy?"

Out of the corner of his eye, John saw the priest nod. "A very good guy," Faust said quietly.

John looked at the road, trying to decide whether Faust could be telling the truth. He had been so convinced that Andrew Card had been one of the Coven himself, but what if he had been wrong? "You said there was a second reason."

Faust stared straight ahead at the road. "They left the body there because they believed it would bring you."

John swerved out of his lane causing the car passing on the left to lay on his horn. John recovered and got back to the right. The other driver flipped him the bird and rocketed past. "At first I thought it might have been my daughter," John said, giving voice to the fear that had nearly torn him in half as he walked into the attic room and first saw the body. "Yes."

John felt his pulse spike. "You know about my daughter?" "We suspected it, but we didn't know for sure."

"What do you know?" John asked, turning toward Faust. "Is Sarah still alive? Who took her?"

Faust nodded toward the road, showing where John should keep his eyes. "I'm sure she is alive. Dead she has no value to the Coven. Alive she is worth a great deal, because through her, they may be able to control you."

"Who took her?" "Jessica Lodge."

"Do you know where she is?"

"We suspect she's been taken out of the country." "Where?"

"England."

"Oh, my God," John said, speaking to himself. "I knew it." Turning to the priest again, he said, "I've got to go get her."

"You need to get her, but you need to be incredibly careful and strategic because the people who oppose you are highly intelligent and dangerous. You also need to know you're not alone. You need to let us plan your daughter's rescue with you."

"*Us?*"

"I'll explain the details shortly."

John shot him an angry glare. "Why not now?"

"Please, I am prepared to give you that information, but only as part of a larger conversation."

John wanted to argue, but he sensed it would do no good. "What did you mean when you said they thought the body would bring me?"

"You have the blood."

"What blood are you talking about?"

"You are John Andrews, descended from Rebecca Nurse on one side and Ann Putnam on the other. I know who you are. I know everything about you."

John stared straight ahead, not liking what he was hearing. "What's that supposed to mean, that you know everything about me?"

"We have studied you."

John felt his temper beginning to fray, but also a cold fear spreading in his stomach. "Who the hell is *we?*"

"All in good time." Faust paused but only for a second. "You sensed him there, didn't you?"

"Who, Andrew Card? I sensed something, but I don't know if it was Card I sensed," John said. Out of the corner of his eye, he could see Faust's head turned toward him. The priest was studying him the way a scientist might see a lab rat.

"It's not a sin that you sensed the body. That part of your blood talks to you as much as the other side."

Unable to concentrate on the road, John swerved again. Another driver honked. He pulled back into his lane and desperately tried to make his mind focus on driving, but his brain was riveted on the fact that the DNA from the Putman side of his family meant that the Coven was alive and well and functioning inside him.

"You have freewill, John," the priest went on. "Nothing about your ancestry can force you to side with evil. The fact that you have not done so and yet while you have a sensitivity to the workings of the Coven makes you a powerful foe. They fear you. They fear you even more because they know what you did to the leaders of the Salem Coven."

John gripped the wheel and stared straight ahead. "Who are you and why were you waiting there in the parking lot?"

"As I said before, explaining exactly who I am will take a while. It's a complicated story. As for why I was there, I felt the same pull you felt, and since I assumed you would be drawn there just as I was, I assumed further that there might be an attempt to kidnap or kill you."

"If they wanted to kill me, why didn't they just come to my house and shoot me?"

"There is something powerful that protects your house.

They would never try to harm you there."

John glanced at Faust. Was he talking about the spirit of Rebecca Nurse? Even though Rebecca had fallen silent and invisible since the night she'd entered his body and together they killed the leaders of the Coven, he wondered if Rebecca Nurse still protected the house. He wondered moreover how Faust knew so much about all of this. "They could have killed me at my office."

Faust shook his head. "The Coven has worked for over three hundred years without anyone else knowing they exist. There aren't even rumors about them, are there?"

John shook his head. Faust was right. Until he'd met the Coven on his own, he'd never had any inkling that such a thing could exist. He had discovered it quite by accident when he started to investigate the reasons the Boston area had so many young people who ran away from home and never heard from again. The disappearances were a story he and Amy had just started digging into about the time Rebecca Nurse first appeared to him. Initially the sight of Rebecca's spirit made him question his sanity, and at the same time he'd had no clue that blood sacrifices by Satan worshippers could have been the cause of the disappearances. John shook his head. Little by little the constant awareness that he was marked for death was wearing him down, making him feel like he was getting closer and closer to the end of his rope. "If they knew I was coming, why didn't they just hide in the cellar at the House of the Seven Gables and kill me there?"

Faust nodded. "They were supposed to do just that, but the Coven makes mistakes, just like everyone else. I'm assuming those two people were late getting here."

John looked at him. "I'm still alive only because of a mistake and a murderous priest?"

Faust pointed ahead, indicating that John should keep his eyes on the road. "Something like that," he said.

PART II

CHAPTER SEVENTEEN

Sarah Andrews opened her eyes and muted sunlight coming through the curtains. She sat up, and as she did, realized the plastic handcuffs had been removed from her wrists. It was the first time they had been free since she was held captive. Moving tentatively, she swung her feet out of bed and found them free of restraints, as well.

She stood, and feeling the chill in the room, reached for the robe that lay on a chair and pulled it on before walking to the window. A recognizable heaviness in her head and limbs told her drugs were still in her system. The feeling was becoming strangely familiar, and she wondered what that meant and what the drugs were and what impact they were having.

She still had enough self-awareness to know her reactions no longer felt normal. She had been kidnapped, and she was sure she was in a foreign country—England judging from the accents of the people who had brought her food and walked her to the bathroom—but unlike her first days here she no longer felt a sense of fear or panic. She felt a gentle lethargy, a lack of caring much about anything.

She turned and looked at the room. It was large, had lofty ceilings and billowy curtains over the large windows, and filled with lovely antiques. Oriental rugs covered the floors and the chairs and couches upholstered in lovely English chintz. The setting was what she would expect to find in an English country house or a luxury boutique hotel.

When she pulled aside the gauzy curtains and gazed down from her window, she could see large formal gardens bounded by a stone wall. Along the wall itself, rose bushes sat covered with burlap against the possibility of frost dam- age, and in the center of the garden the perennial beds had been heavily mulched for winter. Beyond the wall lush green meadows ran to the top of a distant hill.

She could see no other houses, but when she put her head against the glass and looked out to the right, she could make out the roof of what looked like a barn with a riding ring and paddock. To the left she could see a swimming pool, also covered for winter, and a cabana, and beyond it a tennis court. Wherever she was, the setting seemed completely idyllic, the kind of spot that under any normal circumstances she would have wanted to be.

She knew she was a prisoner, of course, but that realization brought no sense of fear, anxiety, or anger, perhaps because she felt so delightfully unintimidated and unthreatened. Also, there seemed to be no pressure, nothing she needed to do, at least she couldn't think of anything. Her job, for years the most important thing in her life, had retreated into the back- ground. She felt no anxiety about her safety, or her job or about her extended absence from it. In short, she knew she didn't seem to be able to summon the energy to care about anything.

She stood looking out the window for a time, her mind empty of further thoughts. In addition to not thinking about work, she did not think about Boston, or her friends. She didn't wonder whether she was reported missing or whether her father and the police were searching for her, or even why people had gone to the trouble to bring her here.

After she had been standing at the window long enough to lose track of time, she heard a noise outside her room, the unmistakable *ting* as pieces of fine China knocked softly together. Then came a soft knock. "Come in," she said, her voice rough and soft from long disuse.

A second later the door opened and a house cleaner wearing a black uniform with white apron and cuffs pushed in a cart loaded with a teakettle, a basket of rolls and breads, a covered platter of scrambled eggs and bacon, a small pitcher of orange juice, a half grapefruit, and a vase of flowers. She wheeled the cart over to a table with two chairs beside one of the windows.

"Breakfast, madam," she said. "Thank you," Sarah answered.

She gave a formal nod and walked out of the room. Sarah stared at her breakfast. and finally summoned the energy to walk over and sit down at the table. She was neither hungry nor thirsty, but she knew she had to eat something to keep up her strength. She picked up a slice of orange with her fingers and put it in her mouth.

A second later she heard another knock at her door. "May I come in?" a woman's voice said.

"Yes."

A second later Jessica Lodge put her head in the door. "Good morning, my dear."

Sarah looked at her. "Good morning." She had known Jessica Lodge for years from events at the paper. She knew Jessica owned the paper, and she knew her father had always been very fond of her. She also knew that in the last phone conversation she'd had with her father, he had hinted that Jessica had done something very wrong, but he hadn't told her what it was. In any case, she no longer cared what it might be.

"How are you feeling this morning?" Jessica asked. "Okay, I guess."

"Good." Jessica gave her a warm smile that suggested she very much hoped it was true. "I know the past days have been very difficult for you," she went on. "I apologize for taking you the way we did and for keeping you here against your will."

"Why did you do it?" Sarah asked, trying to mobilize her intellect enough to care.

"Because there are many things, I need to teach you." "Where are we?"

"Cornwall, England."

Sarah nodded, trying to understand how she had come to be so far from Boston with only the vaguest memory of traveling here. "What do you want to teach me?"

"Things that relate to your ancestors and your abilities, my dear."

"I don't know what you're talking about."

"I know. There are things have been kept from you, things you will come to understand. Things that will change the way you look at the world."

Sarah shook her head. It was so much work to try and follow the conversation. "How will I look at the world?"

"There is a small group of us who understand the true nature of power in the world. Your heritage makes it possible for you to be one of that group, and we would like you to join us. What you are about to learn is going to contradict the things you have known to be true." Jessica smiled again.

Sarah tried to understand what Jessica was talking about. "You make it sound like it's unusual. I'm twenty-eight years old," Sarah said, realizing she was having a challenging time putting complex sentences together. Just having this simple conversation was a struggle. "I'm no child. What can be so strange you can't just tell me?"

Jessica smiled again. "I'm going to rock your world, as they say, but I'm going to do it bit by bit, so I don't blow your mind." She seemed so delighted at her phrases. "Don't I sound hip?" she asked with a laugh.

Jessica pointed to Sarah's breakfast cart. "You must eat up, my dear. Then take a shower and get dressed. I'll come back upstairs to fetch you in an hour, and we'll go into the garden and begin your lessons. Does that sound like a good plan?"

Sarah poured tea into her cup and took a sip. She nodded, thinking that going along with Jessica's suggestions sounded like the most splendid idea in the world.

CHAPTER EIGHTEEN

Father Fast finished his last bit of Irish stew, took a bit of bread, and wiped the last of the gravy from the bowl, and then dabbed his lips with a napkin. "Thank you. That was a fabulous meal. I am in your debt."

Amy smiled at him. "You saved John's life today. I think it's about the least we can do to express our appreciation." Faust nodded and smiled, took a sip of wine, and settled back in his chair. John thought he looked incredibly relaxed for someone who had killed two people and disposed of their bodies in an airport parking lot. If Faust were a priest, as he claimed, John didn't know how an apparent lack of reflection on having taken human lives could go hand in hand with vows. He tried to think back on whether Faust had even said grace at the beginning of the meal, but he couldn't remember.

Earlier in the afternoon, not knowing what else to do, John had brought Faust back to his house and then left him there for a time when he went into the *Salem News*. When he'd gotten there, he'd spoken with Jack Daniels, Lucinda Jenkins, Jackie McKinney, and Tim Monahan, apologizing for his absence from the paper at such a critical time. As soon as he said that they told him that earlier that morning, two Boston police officers had shown up at the paper to ask him questions relating to the missing person's report filed by Sarah's television station. The police visit had served as enough of a reminder of John's personal problems that his absence hadn't upset anyone.

After speaking to the staff, John had taken Amy into his office, closed the door, warned her to keep her expression deadpan and not exclaim, and then he'd told her everything that had happened that morning. They had agreed to meet with Faust together over dinner and make him explain who he was, who he worked for, as well as everything he knew about John and Sarah.

Now, John reached across and refilled the priest's glass with more red wine, eager to loosen the priest's tongue and hear everything Faust had to say. Up to this point, the con- versation had been polite and inconsequential, and each time John had tried to ask more penetrating questions, the priest had deflected. John was struggling to smother his growing anger and frustration, but he also had the impression the priest had been taking his and Amy's measure, just as John

and Amy had been trying to figure out Faust.

The priest was trying to figure out what to tell them, whether they could be trusted with the information he had to impart, whether he needed to be blunt or diplomatic. For his part, John needed information, and he was about to get rude, although the thought also occurred to him that getting rude with an armed killer might not be the best approach.

The priest was in his fifties, John guessed, but he had a wiry body that carried no fat, and he moved with the grace and quickness of a man who was in excellent physical shape. With his short-cropped bristle of gray hair, intense blue eyes, and narrow face, he didn't exactly sup- port the image of a friendly priest. Overall, John thought Faust looked much more like a soldier than a man of religion. In fact, Faust's accent, combined with his crooked nose, suggested it was broken more than once, made John think of a Gestapo officer from an old WWII movie. Throughout the dinner, John had glanced at Amy, and he could sense her wariness of the priest.

To the degree that Faust sensed John and Amy's uneasiness and the questions that were churning in their brains, it didn't seem to create any sense of urgency to explain himself. It was only after Faust had eaten every morsel on his plate and started to sip his freshened glass of wine that he nodded to Amy. "My thanks again for a very lovely dinner."

He turned to John. "Now we need to talk of more serious matters. I know you're eager for answers."

John, barely able to contain his impatience, managed a tight smile. "I was wondering when we were going to get to that," he said, burning to hear everything the man knew about Sarah.

"Are you a religious man?" Faust asked.

"Hardly," John said, swallowing his frustration, but realizing Faust wasn't going to be rushed. "I was raised Catholic, but I've been pretty much an agnostic most of my adult life."

Faust nodded. "And you?" he asked Amy.

"Basically, the same. I was raised in the Lutheran church, but I don't practice."

"Has anything changed for you in the past month?"

John scowled. "I hope this isn't an attempted reintroduction to Catholicism. I want to talk about my daughter."

Faust gave him a hard look. "It's not a reintroduction to religion at all. Please answer my question."

"Well, of course things have changed, but you knew the answer to that question before you asked it."

"How would you explain what happened to you?" "I don't have a goddamn clue."

"Sure, you do."

"Okay, I was invaded by a spirit."

Faust nodded. "We call it 'invested.' It was the spirit of Rebecca Nurse, correct?"

John tightened his lips, but he nodded. "How do you know all this? And who is *we*?"

"I'll answer your questions shortly but before I do, let me ask a few more."

John shook his head and drummed his fingers on the table.

"So did you ever encounter this spirit before it invested you?"

John pursed his lips, but answered, "Yes." "And did she reveal anything to you?" "Yes."

"May I ask what?"

John looked at Amy, his eyes full of anger and frustration, but she gave him an encouraging nod.

"It was very confusing because I had a concussion, but she showed me how to open a secret door that led to the Coven's underground lair. And then she took me on some kind of," he raised his hands to show that he was groping for the right words, "some kind of tour through time."

Faust nodded, encouraging him to go on.

"We went back to the day she was arrested by Edward Putnam and George Corwin, and then we went to a secret meeting between those two and some other people from early Salem when they swore a covenant to worship Satan."

"And then could you please tell me what happened the night you went down into the catacombs to rescue," he tipped his head toward Amy, "you I believe."

Amy nodded, and John went on. "A man who I had believed to be one of my best friends, Rich Harvey, went down with me. I thought he was coming to help me. I had no idea that he was trying to deliver me to the Coven."

"And what happened when you got to wherever you were going?"

"There was a room, like a paneled dining room with mahogany walls and oriental rugs, and the leaders of the Coven were sitting around a table like they were just having a nice dinner, but there was a big door that opened onto this other room." John closed his eyes and shook his head, and he saw Amy's face go pale as she was reminded of the same thing. "I know this is very difficult," Faust prodded. "But it's also especially important. Please go on."

"The walls and floor of this room were white tile, like a shower room. Shackles were set in the walls, and I could see two people—they looked like teenagers. They were naked and dead, and their bodies had been terribly disfigured." John took a deep breath. "The walls and the floor were smeared with so much blood... and then I also saw Amy. She too was shackled. Cabby Corwin, a Salem police officer, was starting to torture her."

John bowed his head and closed his eyes, wishing he could permanently erase every vestige of memory from that horrible night.

"What impressions did you have?" Faust asked.

John looked up. "What are you talking about!" he snapped. "What impressions? Are you joking? I wanted to kill those people!"

Faust held up a calming hand, and Amy reached across and took John's wrist and squeezed.

"Did the members of the Coven appear to fear you when you first walked in?"

John tried to remember, and after a second he shook his head. "They seemed pleased, like they were feeling very cocky and thought they had somehow beaten me."

Faust nodded and smiled. "I'm sure they did. But can you tell me what happened next?"

"My friend Rich hit me over the head, and when I came to, I was shackled in the tile room."

"And?"

"What I said before. When Corwin started to torture Amy, I felt my anger spike like it had never spiked before. I felt, I don't know, *different*, like I was split into two parts. One part was fear; the other part was pure rage. And then I looked over and saw Rebecca Nurse holding my hand. She told me something she had told me before, but I'd never understood."

"And what was that?" Faust asked. "That *I was the weapon*."

Faust nodded, and John could feel the man's intensity rising, like heat from a fireplace. "Okay," Faust prodded. "What happened next?"

"I felt Rebecca flow into me, but then I felt something else, and I looked to my left and saw this other spirit, and I knew who she was."

Faust's eyes went a little wider. "Yes, go on."

"It was a local girl named Melissa Blake who'd disappeared, and I felt her flow into me."

Faust was looking at him much more intently suddenly. "Say that again. Think back and try to be clear. You felt invested by a second presence?"

John nodded. "Yes."

Faust nodded, squinting slightly as if he was suddenly skeptical. "And then what happened."

"I had been shackled to the wall, like I said, but when both spirits came into me, the shackles exploded."

"You're quite sure of that."

"I know what an explosion looks like." "Sorry, it's just that details are important."

"I'm not sure why that detail is any more important that the rest. If I told these things to anybody else, they'd put me on Thorazine."

Faust folded his hands on the table and gave John a look that made him fall silent. "I fully expected you to tell me the spirit of Rebecca Nurse invested you, but I did not expect you to tell me about the second spirit. You should not have been able to break out of those shackles, even with one spirit investing you, and maybe not even with two."

"There's more. There's one thing I forgot." Faust's eyebrows went up again. "Yes?"

"When Melissa Blake held my left hand, it wasn't just her. I could see a whole chain of other spirits linking their hands to hers. The line went on and on. I couldn't count them all, but I knew who they were. They were other people who had been killed by the Coven over the years."

"You actually *saw* this?"

John nodded.

"How did you feel?"

"Incredibly powerful, like I had power inside me that, if I'd just let it go at once, would have blown up the whole city block above us."

"Dear God," Faust said to himself.

"What?" Amy asked.

"Astounding. This explains so much."

CHAPTER NINETEEN

The table was and the most unusual shape she had ever seen. It looked like a hexagon, but instead of having points, each spoke of the hexagon ended in an inward curve so that someone could pull up a chair and nestle into the nook. A tablecloth covered and six candelabras, with six candles each, set the tone for the room.

Seven other people sat at the table along with Sarah, each of them at the end of one of the spokes, except for the one spoke where Jessica Lodge sat beside another person, a man. Sarah sat along the side of the spoke nearest Jessica Lodge. She wore a white dress with long sleeves and a high collar. Her hair was pulled back tightly, in a bun, something she would never have chosen herself.

The others at the table were dressed in all black, in similar formal clothing. They were all quite a bit older than Sarah, in their sixties or seventies, she guessed. Jessica Lodge wore a long black dress with a swirl of black sequins that went from her shoulder to her hip. Around her neck she wore a necklace with a ruby pendant the size of a thumbnail. She looked as regal as a visiting queen. Beside her sat a man with wavy white hair, a prominent nose as straight as a ruler, a chin that jutted like the prow of a ship, and steely eyes that made him look like someone who had been in command of others all his life.

The other women, of whom there were two, had neatly coiffed gray hair, equally expensive jewelry, and long gowns. The men were all distinguished. They had features typified by tight skin over good bones, and pampered faces that suggested they were accustomed to a certain amount of wealth, power, and control, and they wore tuxedos and starched shirts.

The aura around the table was so stilted and formal that Sarah felt like a little girl going through a church confirmation ceremony. The part of her brain that was coherent thought this whole thing was ridiculous and that she ought to get up and excuse herself, but there was a part of her that found it easy just to go along. They were sitting in a dining room, but it wasn't the formal dining room on the first floor of the large country house where Jessica and Sarah were staying. This room was in the basement, at the bottom of a narrow staircase. She had the sense that few visitors to the house knew this room existed. Sarah wondered why anyone would have such a lovely dining room underground and so far from a kitchen. Her mind wandered. Did Jessica own this house? She felt like she did, which was odd because she had always been under the impression that Jessica lived in Salem.

The well-honed TV-news-journalist part of Sarah's mind produced those kinds of thoughts and asked those kinds of questions, but it had to work *so* hard because the larger part of her mind felt like a dry sponge, and it just accepted all this as normal. Sarah felt the same sluggishness she'd felt for days, as if pushing thoughts through her brain was like sucking molasses through a straw.

At times, the TV-news-journalist part of her brain would become alarmed and try to tell her that she ought to be frightened because things were happening to her that were out of her control. But those thoughts were so hard to hold on to. Her thoughts and emotions were buried beneath the steady blizzard of other sensations: heaviness, comfort, a feeling of wellbeing. It was so much easier to simply take everything in and not fight it, but to let it accumulate.

Sometimes she imagined she was lying in the sand at the edge of a very warm ocean where the things Jessica Lodge had been telling her were like waves surging onto a beach and washing over her like the gentlest intrusion, and then receding back and heading out to sea again. The part of her brain that accepted Jessica's idea also accepted the strange symbols inlaid in the dining room's mahogany paneled walls, and it didn't wonder if they were weird or even sinister, which the other part of her mind tried to suggest. The accepting part of her brain listened and absorbed the rite that had been per- formed by the man sitting beside Jessica Lodge. He was Lord somebody or other, she couldn't recall the name, which she had heard when they first sat down. The man had mumbled his words in the stilted cadence of a prayer, but it hadn't really been a prayer, at least not the kind of prayer she had ever heard before.

The same man had been addressing her, his voice dull and oddly monotone, and it made her feel even heavier than she'd felt before. He was telling her about the beliefs these people shared and their "congregation," as he called it. He said their membership was small and very select, and that the "one they worshipped," as he put it, had rewarded them richly over the centuries with power, wealth, and long and healthy lives.

Sarah wasn't listening to what he said, at least not the way she would listen to a news account if she were at work, where she would question and evaluate and weigh the facts. Instead, she was *absorbing* what the man said to her to a degree. The questioning part of her brain wondered what that meant, what it was doing to her. The larger part of her brain sensed it coming in and didn't care.

CHAPTER TWENTY

"I'm glad it explains so much to you, "John exclaimed sarcastically before his tone turned to ice. "Now tell me what you know about my daughter."

"I understand your impatience, but I beg your forbearance. There are reasons we need to cover this information."

John closed his eyes. They'd had a late dinner to start with, and now it was getting late. He wanted information about Sarah, and he wanted it *now*; only the fact that this man had saved his life induced him to be patient. "Go on."

"You said the Coven leaders seemed very confident," Faust said.

John nodded.

"That's because you never should have been able to break the shackles."

"But Rebecca Nurse—"

"Not you *and* Rebecca Nurse, and not even you both and Melissa Blake. I'm certain those restraints were reinforced specifically to hold you."

"How does any of this relate to Sarah?" John asked. "Do you remember that when we started talking, I asked if either of you were deeply religious. I asked because I wanted to know if you were doubters and skeptics, and you are. It makes what I need to tell you easier to accept than it might if you identify with a particular theology."

Faust looked back and forth between John and Amy. "Would it surprise you to know I am a Catholic priest, but I collaborate with people from every other major religion; moreover, if what I do were to be made known the public, the Pope would completely repudiate me?"

John shook his head. "I have no idea what you're getting at. The only thing that matters, at least to me, is my daughter!"

Faust's eyes became hard and for the first time they sparked with anger. "I'm sorry to tell you that this is much bigger than your daughter, or you or Amy or me or any of us. This is about the ultimate battle of good versus evil. God versus Satan. That battle is real, and it's enjoined by all the world's major religions. Fighting Satan is the core of our mission. The battle is active and all around us. No religion acknowledges it, but we are all engaged in the fight, and you more than anyone else has personal experience to understand what I'm talking about. As painful as it may be, you need to understand that while I am dedicated to helping you get your daughter back; her abduction is part of something much larger. And under no circumstances will I do anything that weakens our ability to win the larger battle."

"You expect us to believe that you, along with—what—a bunch of rabbis and imams and Buddhist monks, are part of some secret organization that unites all the religions to fight Satan?"

Faust nodded. "Exactly."

"You're supposed to be, like, religious commandos, huh?" "Exactly."

"What about all the fundamentalists out there, the Muslims who believe in jihad; the fundamental Christians who believe that the Bible is the absolute word of God and Jesus is the only possible path to salvation? What do they think of you?"

"We've worked very hard to keep our existence secret." "Even from people within your own religion?"

Faust nodded. "The people who claim to be fundamentalists are undercover operators for the Coven. Their secret mission is to destabilize all the forces of good, and what better way to achieve their ends than by tearing religions apart and dividing people under the guise that they're holier than everyone else?"

John shook his head.

"You doubt what I'm telling you?"

"Well, you say the Coven worships evil, which means they worship destruction, right?" Faust nodded.

"What happens when they win? Everything blows up, right, including them?"

Faust smiled. "The leaders of the Coven are the ultimate cynics. They worship the forces of destruction, but they believe the battle between God and Satan is eternal, and that neither one will win. They also believe that Satan will reward them richly for their loyalty, and he has. The forces of evil are powerful and extremely wealthy, and they're worldwide."

"Amy and I are just a couple of newspaper editors in a small city in Massachusetts. I don't see how we figure into this global struggle you describe."

Faust's expression became hard again. "You know very well how you figure in. You, who have the blood of the Nurses *and* the Putnam's flowing in your veins and descended from both sides in this struggle. You have an innate sensitivity to evil as well as to good. That's why you got into the coven's catacombs in the first place. It was no accident that Rebecca Nurse chose you."

"Are you saying my ancestry makes it possible that I could have chosen to join the Coven?"

Faust nodded. "Certainly. As a boy, if you had shown the right characteristics, they might have approached you back then. The Coven is incredibly careful whom they contact. Just having the right blood is not enough; a candidate must display the right attitude."

John felt a flush of guilt at Faust's insistence that he could have chosen evil over good, and for a moment he had to look away from the priest's frank blue eyes. It was something he

wanted to deny, but at the same time he had always known the pull was there. He recalled events in his youth when he had shoplifted or engaged in vandalism or gotten into fights. Something like a siren song had sounded in his blood, and even at the time it had frightened him because he'd recognized it as a lust for more risk, bigger thrills, more violence. The same song had been there again when his wife had been killed and its lure had whispered strongly to him during the times, he'd been in the worst grip of alcohol abuse and depression. Then, like a call to come to the edge of the cliff, to put the barrel of the gun into his mouth, it had lured him toward the darkness, promised him that his pain would all disappear if he would just end things.

Even now, as he looked back at those times, he wondered what small thing had made him reject the siren song and turn away from the darkness. Each time whatever had allowed him to be strong had, at the time, seemed so small and insignificant. Each time it had been one ephemeral factor in an unconscious decision tree, but whatever had kept him going in the right direction, a badly flawed man somehow making the right choice.

He was staring down at the table when he felt a strong grip on his wrist. He looked up in surprise to see that Father Faust had grabbed him. "It's nothing to be ashamed of," Faust said. "We *all* feel it, and we need to acknowledge it. All of us who can be soldiers in this war *have* to feel it. We understand the pull of darkness; we feel the desire to give into it, but we don't. We find the strength to resist, and that is the first step. It is a huge first step.

"The second step is to learn to use our strength to fight back. When you became invested by the spirit of Rebecca Nurse, you were learning to use your innate strength."

John shook his head. "I was out of my mind with rage and fear. Rebecca Nurse did all the work."

"However, it happened, it happened. You were also able to invest yourself with the spirit of Melissa Blake and with the spirits of other victims."

John kept shaking his head. "You don't understand. I didn't *do* anything. I just let it happen." He looked away, intimidated by the fact that Faust understood things about him he had never admitted to any other human being. It gave him a sense that he was being put under a microscope, and it made him uncomfortable "What about Amy?" he asked, wanting to change the subject.

Faust turned toward her. "Through your ancestors, each of you has a hereditary attachment to this age-old battle, but Amy's is different. John holds a strong linkage to both evil *and* good. Amy has a strong linkage to good. She is descended from Giles Corey, the only man who resisted the urging of the Salem judges to confess or give a plea. As you both know, a person accused of witchcraft could only be tried for their crime when they made a plea—either guilty or innocent, it didn't matter. A person who was found guilty had all their property seized. If they did not make a plea, they could not be tried, and their property could not be taken. It was no accident that the sheriff and the judges ended up with all that seized property. To induce people to make a plea, they were threatened with being "pressed," which meant being slowly crushed beneath a suffocating mass of heavy stones until they made their plea.

"Amy's ancestor was the only person who had the strength of character to resist making a plea, and thus he died after days of being crushed beneath a load of stones. Amy has aspects of his strength. It is a powerful asset in this fight, and the fact that the two of you have been drawn together makes the combination of her strength and your unique talents a potent alliance."

John shook his head, wanting to reject all of this. He wanted to be left alone. He wanted to make a strong drink, sit by the fire, and read a book until he fell asleep. He wanted no part of this struggle. He just wanted to get Sarah back.

As if she was sensing his weakness, Amy reached across the table and took his hand. The moment he felt her touch something flowed into him, and he recognized that she was sharing her strength with him.

"Father Faust is right, John. Remember, I was the only other one who could see the names scarred into your arm. We are together for a reason, and we're stronger together than we are apart."

Feeling the truth of her words, John closed his eyes and nodded.

"Remember what Rebecca Nurse told you, John," Amy went on. "*You are the weapon.*"

"Yes," Faust said, "and now that brings us to your daughter."

CHAPTER TWENTY-ONE

B racing for unwelcome news, John grabbed Amy's hand.

"As I said before," Faust said quickly, "I'm quite certain she is alive. The Coven needs her alive, so they have a source of control over you. It makes no strategic sense to kill her."

"You said she may be in England."

Faust nodded. "We think Jessica Lodge flew her there." "Where in England?"

"Almost certainly in Cornwall." "Why Cornwall?"

"Because it's as important to the Coven as Salem." "Why is Salem so important? History?"

"The House of the Seven Gables is here." John laughed. "So what? It's a house Nathaniel Hawthorne used in a novel. That's the only reason anybody cares about it."

Faust shook his head. "That's what the Coven would like you to think. The House of the Seven Gables has a fundamental importance to them."

Amy had been quiet the entire time, but now she sat forward. "Why?"

Faust grimaced helplessly. "We're not certain. It could simply be symbolic value, but we believe it's more than that." He shook his head. "We believe the presence of the house has meaning. It's the shape of the house. There's something inside the house we don't know about."

Amy nodded. "Recently there were a bunch of letters and other documents found in the House of the Seven Gables. They're at the Phillips Library, and John has seen them."

John shrugged. "I've been over there going through them twice in the past two weeks. The first time I saw Nathaniel Hawthorne's writing he'd wanted kept secret until after his death." He looked at Faust. "Hawthorne knew about the Coven. His is ancestors had been members. He wanted the world to know about the Coven, but he feared retaliation against himself or his family, so he wanted the papers hidden until after his death.

"Then just yesterday I was at the Phillips Museum again, and I saw a handful of letters written from someone in England to a woman named Elizabeth Turner. I'm certain she was the wife of Captain John Turner, who originally built the first part of what later became known as the House of the Seven Gables. After I read the letter, I found another page it was in the same envelope. That page didn't have any writing, but instead it had a drawing of a house remarkably like the House of the Seven Gables. It wasn't the same house, it had lines drawn from the gables. A second drawing showed the house as a point in the world with the lines radiating out and going everywhere."

Faust's eyes narrowed, and John saw an eager gleam. "Can you show me that document?" Faust asked.

"I'll take you first thing in the morning."

Faust glanced at his watch. "Then I need to get some sleep."

He stood and took his plate to the kitchen, where he helped Amy and John load the dishwasher. Afterward, they walked him to the front door. "Where are you staying?" Amy asked.

"The Hawthorne Hotel."

"I'll pick you up at nine," John said.

He walked Faust out onto the sidewalk, shivering in the dampness. Glancing overhead, he saw a thick layer of low clouds covering the sky, and he felt a penetrating dampness that threatened rain or an early snow. He started down the street with Faust, intending to go with the priest to Derby Street to flag a taxi, and that was when he spotted the movement. It was subtle, hardly anything more than a shadow moving a little more than it should have.

John said nothing, but he turned his head slightly so he could keep watching through his peripheral vision. The movement had come from a car parked just down the street, and when he looked more carefully, two heads were barely visible through the tinted glass. Even as his now-familiar sense of paranoia flashed, the rational part of his brain tried to squelch it. Salem was a big tourist spot, he told himself. Even though Halloween had just passed, there would still be plenty of visitors in town. The two people could very possibly be a man and a woman who had just met that evening in one of the nearby bars. They could be two old friends who hadn't seen each other in a long time, or a young couple having an argument.

But they could also be two killers sent by the Coven.

Operating purely on instinct but realizing that at this point paranoia could save his life, John grabbed Faust's arm. "On second thought, why don't you stay at my house tonight?" he said.

Faust looked at him and seeming to recognize the intensity in John's expression, nodded and didn't try to fight or argue as John turned him around and they started walking quickly back the way they'd come. John saw Faust's hand snake into his coat pocket where he knew the priest kept his pistol.

"What was that about?" Faust asked as John unlocked the front door and ushered him back inside.

"I saw two people in a car outside." He shook his head. "I just didn't like it."

"A gut feeling?" Faust asked without any trace of mockery or humor.

John nodded.

"Listen to your gut."

"I try to." John went upstairs into his office and a second later came down with his Browning .45. He checked to make sure the clip was full then jacked a shell into the chamber.

"I don't think you're going to need that," Faust said. "What makes you so sure?"

"The Coven would have attacked this house long ago if they thought they could get away with it. Whether the spirit of Rebecca Nurse is gone, as you suspect, or whether it is still here, they believe the house is protected. That, plus what you did to their leaders means they will not confront you directly, especially in a place where you can draw strength. The Coven is small in numbers, and they work in secrecy and darkness. They are not risk takers."

Faust's words reminded John of what he had done to the leaders of the Coven, and he unconsciously flexed his fists. Would that power be there again if he needed it? He wondered because he certainly couldn't feel it now, nor had he felt even a hint of it again since the one time he used it in the Coven's catacombs. Since he hadn't understood what happened at the time, and since he really didn't understand it any better now, all he knew for sure was that he couldn't control it, and he had no reason to believe he would ever be able to call on those powers again.

He clicked the safety on and shoved the big automatic pistol into his belt. "Better safe than sorry," he said.

CHAPTER TWENTY-TWO

S arah shivered in the freezing morning air then buried her hands in the big pockets of the old Barbour coat and pulled her arms in tight to her body for warmth. The clouds were low overhead and heavy with moisture. The air was full of fog and dampness that rolled in off the ocean. Sarah couldn't see the water from here, but she knew it was near because she felt its humid presence and smelled brine in the air, just the way she had all her life in Salem.

Jessica Lodge knew what Sarah was thinking because she turned her head toward the sky and sniffed. "You can smell the salt, can't you?"

Sarah nodded. "I can tell we're near the ocean."

Jessica pointed to their left, then straight ahead and then again to their right. "Just a few miles in almost all directions," she said.

Sarah stopped walking. They had come out a door at the rear of the large house, walked through the formal gardens that Sarah could see from her bedroom window, and then gone out a garden gate and headed through a path that led to a dirt lane. It was the second day she and Jessica had taken a walk after breakfast.

They went along the lane for twenty minutes, in companionable silence, when Sarah turned to Jessica again. "This is a bit embarrassing, but how long have I been here? I know that's a crazy question, but I feel like I've lost track of time. Just this morning I was thinking about my job, and I realized I haven't thought about it for days."

Jessica gave her a gentle smile. "Do you want to leave?" "No!" Sarah said quickly, trying to understand the confusion she was feeling. "I've loved being here, but I'm feeling like a little bit like Alice in Wonderland, as if I've tumbled into a hole and fallen out of the world."

Jessica laughed and linked her arm through Sarah's. "You needed a vacation far more than you realized. I've spoken to people at your television network and explained that you are with me here in England and that you are making important contacts that will give you invaluable access to some significant stories. And that, my dear, is true. The people you met last night at dinner are going to be of foremost importance going forward. And you are going to have personal access to all of them."

Jessica laughed gently. "Trust me when I tell you, the world of the future is going to look a great deal different than the world you have known growing up. The people I know, the movers and shakers who work outside the eye of public scrutiny, have been putting things in place years now. The world is preparing to change radically, and you, my dear, are going to have the inside track on reporting and interpreting these changes to the rest of humanity. It's going to be an exciting time."

Sarah nodded, flushing with pleasure at the idea that she had selected for such an honor and wondering why she had felt even the slightest misgiving about being away from work for so long. She was learning and meeting people, and just as importantly, someone as important as Jessica Lodge was taking her under her wing and telling her that *this* was where she *needed* to be. That should have been good enough to overcome any anxiety she was feeling. "Thank you for giving me the opportunity."

"You are more qualified for this than you know."

CHAPTER TWENTY-THREE

The next morning John, Amy and Faust ate an early breakfast and left the house together right after- wards. As he exited his front door, John looked around the street, relieved to see the world bathed in early morning light that somehow removed much of the threat he'd felt the night before. Off to his left at the end of his street, he could see the harbor glittering cold and unyielding. Overhead gulls cried, and to his right the city of Salem was waking up, as delivery trucks rumbled through the intersection.

Glancing around at his immediate block, John saw only a row of parked cars, none of which were the one he had seen the night before with the two people sitting inside, and no one else on the street other than one of his neighbors walking a basset hound. Trying to silence the question that popped into his mind as to whether his long-time neighbor was secretly a member of the Coven. He waved to the man as he led Amy and Father Faust to his Audi, which was parked half a block from his house.

John clicked the locks and was about the climb into the car when Faust said, "Just a second."

John turned to see Faust squatting at the trunk, looking underneath the car, and then running his hands along the inside of the bumper.

"Would you please open the hood? But don't start the engine," Faust said.

John climbed into the car, pulled the hood release, and watched as Faust gave the engine a quick check. After a second he closed the hood, came around, and climbed into the rear. "Okay," he said.

John glanced at Faust in the rearview mirror. "Were you looking for bombs?"

"Yes," Faust replied. "Just like you said last night, better safe than sorry."

John felt his stomach tighten as he clicked his seatbelt, started the engine, and pulled away from the curb, and he was thinking that he had never appreciated what it was like to live every day without feeling like a hunted man. Every afternoon, an anxious dread now began to grip him as evening darkness approached, and he had started looking at every single person on the street with suspicion, as if they might be a potential enemy. He realized that the easy feeling of wellbeing he'd enjoyed for so many years might be something he would never experience again.

John gripped the wheel tightly and felt the reassuring lump of the .45 he had jammed into his belt before he walked out of the house. He shook his head as he drove the short distance to the Philips Library at the Peabody Essex Institute, thinking that Massachusetts was one of the strictest states in the union where gun laws were concerned, and here he was with a concealed handgun and no permit. He felt like an accident looking for a place to happen.

"You think anybody will be there this early?" Amy asked. John shrugged. "Joe D'Angelo was there this time yesterday. I'm hoping he's a creature of habit."

He hadn't tried to call D'Angelo the previous evening or that morning because he feared after his visit just a day earlier, D'Angelo would refuse his request to see the boxes of old documents from the House of the Seven Gables again. He was hoping that if he just showed up on the library's doorstep at the same time, D'Angelo would find it harder to refuse his request.

They drove through the light traffic in silence, each of them alone with their thoughts. John glanced at Amy, but she kept her eyes on the road straight ahead. Her lips pursed, and he could see tightness around the eyes he recognized as a combination of stress and concentration. He couldn't help but wonder whether she was reexamining the idea of getting involved with a man marked for death by the Coven.

If she were, he knew he couldn't blame her, because who in their right mind wanted a life spent looking over their shoulder every single moment? The previous night as sleep refused to come he had lain in bed beside her staring up at the ceiling and wondering how his own existence had come to such a pass, with a death threat held over his head, his daughter abducted, and constant suspicion bubbling in his guts that almost every single person around him might be a member of the Coven.

When they pulled into the lot at the Peabody Essex Institute they climbed out and walked across the deserted grounds toward the library. Wind blew across the dead grass, tearing the last brown oak leaves from the trees.

John checked his watch as he led the way up the steps of Plummer Hall. Ten to eight. The library wasn't supposed to open for another hour and ten minutes, but D'Angelo had been there at this hour a day earlier, even though the two of them had been the only two people in the library. Now John just had to hope D'Angelo was a creature of consistent habits.

He looked inside and felt a flush of dismay as he saw that there were very few lights burning, and those that were, looked like they would be on all night. He rapped on the door and then waited a minute or two, pulling his coat tight to his throat to keep the wind from working its way inside. When he saw no one moving inside, he rapped again, and then, as an afterthought, he tried the door to see if D'Angelo had come to work and left the door unlocked for his co-workers.

To his delight, the door swung inward, and he waved Amy and Faust in behind him. They walked into the main library, and their footsteps echoed on the polished wood floors as they looked around in the dimness to try and spot D'Angelo or any of the other librarians.

"Hello?" John called. "Is anybody here?" He paused and waited, and for a second he thought he heard distant foot- steps, so he called out a second time.

Getting no response either time and thinking D'Angelo might be down working on the collection in the rare books section, John led the way through the small side door and down the staircase to the sign that read "Rare Books and Manuscripts Sections. Restricted Access."

John knew the room was locked and could only be accessed with a magnetic key card, and he remembered seeing a buzzer beside the lock that would enable visitors to summon one of the librarians to let them inside. John pushed the buzzer repeatedly and stood back, hoping D'Angelo would soon open the door.

He turned to look at Amy and Faust as they came down the last steps and joined him outside the locked door. Amy was the one who noticed it. She glanced down at the floor by John's feet and pointed. "Is that blood?"

John stepped back and looked down. Where he had been standing the floor was smeared with something dark and red that made the soles of his shoes tacky. His heart went into his mouth, and he was just reaching behind his back for the .45 in his belt when the door to the rare books section jerked open from the inside.

Joe D'Angelo stood there blinking at him through bleary eyes, his cut scalp dripping blood down the side of his face. The rare books curator's arms were braced against the wall to help him stay on his feet, and as soon as he had the door open, he brought the handkerchief he was clutching in his right hand back to the cut on his head to try and staunch the flow of blood.

"Help me," D'Angelo whispered, and he took a step for- ward and collapsed into John's arms.

John took D'Angelo under the arms and together with Faust they managed to get him up the stairs and into the main reading room, while Amy whipped out her cell phone and called 911. By the time other people had reported in for work in the main part of the library, and they helped get D'Angelo to a table where he sat and rested his head on his folded arms.

John sat down beside him at the table. "Don't go to sleep," he warned.

"Easy for you to say," Joe mumbled. "Seriously," John insisted. "Sit up."

Joe sat up, and on his other side one of the other librarians, a heavyset woman in her late fifties, dabbed his head with damp paper towels to clean off the blood while someone else brought ice wrapped in a towel and laid it against his cut. What happened?" John asked when the bustling settled down again.

D'Angelo shook his head. "Somebody snuck up behind me and hit me. I left the door unlocked, and they must have just walked in after I got here."

"After they hit you, what did they do?"

"Dragged me into the rare books area and left me in the little room where we keep the gloves and sweaters. They went on into the collection and came out a minute later carrying something, I think. I was barely conscious and could hardly see.

John felt the anxiety building in his guts again. "Do you have any idea what they took?"

"I can't be sure until I have a chance to check, but I think it was those three boxes of new papers you were looking at yesterday." D'Angelo shook his head and mumbled something else.

"What was that?" John asked. "I can't understand what you just said."

"I said it doesn't make any sense to take those boxes, not when we've got Audubon's and a Guttenberg Bible and lots of other books that are worth so much money."

John sat back and looked up at Amy and Faust who had been waiting behind his chair. "Yes, it does," he said under his breath.

CHAPTER TWENTY-FOUR

Soon they were back at John's house gathered around the breakfast table drinking a fresh pot of coffee. John was hunched over with his elbows on the table and his head cradled in his hands. He leaned forward and stared at the worn and scarred mahogany.

"They broke in and stole the three boxes. It had to be because of the drawing and the Elizabeth Turner letters. I'm certain of it."

"Weren't there a lot of other documents in those boxes beside those letters?"

"Yes, but everything else was straightforward. I mean, they might have wanted the Hawthorne journal, as well, but nothing was like the Elizabeth Turner letters. They were so cryptic."

"Is there any chance the library would have made copies?"

Suddenly John looked up at her and then he slapped his hand hard on the tabletop. "God, what an ass I am!" He jammed his hand in his pocket and came out with his cell phone. "I forgot I'd taken a picture of the letter and the drawing." He clicked on his photo file and started paging through to the most recent pictures. "I didn't think I was supposed to photograph anything, but Joe D'Angelo left me alone, so I took a couple shots."

He found the photos, then stood and hurried upstairs to his desk where he woke up his computer and plugged in the phone. A couple of moments later all three of them were looking at a large image of the drawings he had photographed.

Faust squinted hard at the drawing of the house and the lines that came from it, running outward from each of the gables. Then he looked at the map of the world drawn below.

"What is it?" Amy asked.

Faust shook his head. "I think it's part of a map."

"Where would the rest of the map be?" John asked. "I have no idea."

"What's it a map of?"

Faust was quiet, and then he shook his head again. "Sorry, I don't know." He took a sip of his coffee and turned away from the computer. "What I do know is you need to get over to England as quickly as possible. I don't know what the Coven is planning or why this map was so important to them, but we can't allow any more time to pass. We need to move."

Amy stiffened. "Wait a minute. We have no idea what we're doing. If we go over there, we don't know who or what we're facing. I think it's crazy to just rush in."

Faust spun toward her; his face suddenly twisted with anger. "And if you don't rush in, John's daughter is liable to die!" He jerked his thumb toward John. "Ask him if he's willing wait any longer!"

"Amy," John said. "I have no choice. I must go." "No, you don't," Amy shot back. "Not like this!"

The sound of the doorbell made all three of their heads turn toward the staircase. "Who could that be?" Amy asked. "No idea," John said as he reached into his belt for his .45. He went quickly down the stairs and tiptoed over to stand just to the side of the door. "Who's there?" he asked.

"My name is Lisa Giles."

"What do you want?" he asked, glancing over his shoulder in time to see Amy and Faust coming down the stairs then heading back toward the kitchen.

"I'm sorry to disturb you, but I'd like to talk to you, Mr. Andrews."

"About?"

"About what I think is our common problem?"

John's heart started to beat faster. "What problem is that?" he asked, then held his breath, half expecting bullets to start coming through the door, but not expecting the next words. "The Coven," Lisa Giles said in a faint voice.

John looked back at Amy and Father Faust, raising his eyebrows in question. Amy shrugged, and they both stepped out of sight. John paused, and then holding the pistol down by his leg, he reached over and opened the door.

For a second nothing happened, and then a woman stepped into the opening. She was small and slightly built, late forties or early fifties, John thought, with curly brown hair, big glasses, and nervous, birdlike movements. Her gaze quickly dropped from his face to his hands. Her eyes widened when she saw the gun. "I'm not a threat, Mr. Andrews." She nodded. "I assume you *are* Mr. Andrews?"

John nodded and closed the door behind her, turning the deadbolt as he did. "You said we have a common problem." Lisa Giles stiffened as Amy and Father Faust stepped out from where they had been hiding around the corner. Faust had unbuttoned his coat, and his Roman collar was visible.

Lisa Giles scowled.

"I didn't know you had one of *them* here," she said. "I'll come back another time." She turned and reached for the doorknob.

"Hold, witch!" Faust cried, his voice cracking like a whip.

John looked at the priest in amazement then froze when he saw Faust's gun. It was aimed at the woman. John swore he could see Faust tightening his finger on the trigger.

He held up his hand. "Are you crazy? No!"

Without even thinking about what he was about to do he stepped sideways, blocking Faust's clear shot, and he closed his eyes and tensed, waiting for the impact of a bullet.

A second passed, then two. When John opened his eyes, what he saw next shocked him even more than the sight of Faust's gun. Amy had stepped right behind Faust and had a large chef's knife she must have snatched from the knife block in the kitchen held tight to Faust's throat. John could see the handle of a second knife in Amy's left hand that was prodding the priest in the kidney.

"Drop the gun," Amy hissed.

Faust's eyes were white with shock and fear. "You don't know what you're doing," he snarled. "She's, our enemy!"

"Don't move, and don't say another word. Just drop the gun."

Faust's face twisted with helpless fury, but he did as Amy commanded. His gun clattered to the floor.

"Now kick it toward John," Amy snapped. Faust hesitated, then did as she ordered. "John, pick up the gun," Amy said.

For a second John didn't move, he gaped at her open mouthed. She was acting different from the woman he thought he knew.

"John!" Amy snapped.

He snapped out of his trance, went over, and picked up Faust's gun. Once he did, Amy took the knives away and shoved Faust forward.

With a blade no longer at his throat, Faust recovered. He looked at John, his expression filled with incomprehension. "I saved your life, and you treat me like this!"

"You were going to shoot this woman!" John shouted back. "What were you thinking?"

"She's a *witch!*"

Behind Faust Amy nodded. "Yes, she is, and you're a member of ODX, aren't you?"

John held up a hand for silence, and then he looked between Faust and Lisa Giles, who hadn't said a word since Faust pulled his gun. Unlike Faust, who was full of wild emotions, Lisa Giles seemed understandably shaken yet remarkably calm. She was such a small, mousy woman; he was amazed she wasn't a trembling wreck.

"Are you one of them?" he asked her, "I'm not sure what you mean,"

Giles said. "I *am* a witch, but I am not part of the Salem Coven. They are my enemy, just as they are yours."

John turned to Faust. "What is ODX?"

Faust pressed his lips together and glared at John. "The group that saved your life," he said.

"You've heard of Opus Dei, haven't you, John?" Amy asked.

"Aren't those the guy's Dan Brown wrote that great thriller years ago?"

"Yes, but the real Opus Dei isn't as controversial as Brown made them sound; however, there's an offshoot of Opus Dei called ODX, which is far more radical."

"We believe the world is engaged in a titanic struggle between good and evil," Faust interrupted. "If you think it's radical to battle the Devil, then yes, we're radical."

"But that's not all you battle, is it?" Amy shot back. "You believe that all other religions besides Christianity pose an equal threat, don't you?"

John shook his head. "Father Faust told us that his group is allied with all the other religions."

"It's a lie," Amy said. "Isn't it, Father Faust?"

Faust's eyes were going back and forth between John and Amy. Finally, he settled on John. "This woman," jerking his head toward Lisa Giles, "is a Wiccan. Wiccans use *magic*," he said, pronouncing the word as if magic was something unimaginably filthy and evil. "They believe in a bunch of *spirits*, including their horned god—and if he isn't the Devil, what is he?" Faust was nodding as he spoke. "The Wiccans are the Devil's agents."

Lisa Giles cleared her throat. "May I say something?" she asked in what struck John as a remarkably calm tone given the moments earlier Faust had been preparing to shoot her.

"Go ahead."

"I *am* a witch, and I am a member of a local coven of thirteen witches."

On hearing this Faust recoiled, as if proximity would somehow stain his soul.

Giles went on. "It is true we believe in a number of spirits, and it is also true that we attempt to work magic."

"*See!*" Faust shot back. "I *told* you. These people are dangerous. Magic is the Devil's work."

"Every good lie has as much truth in it as possible," Lisa Giles went on, ignoring Faust. "There really are people from all the world religions who have united in the struggle against the Satanists, but ODX is not part of that group."

"Don't listen to her," Faust growled.

"I would think you would agree that the use of magic is not inherently evil," Giles went on, speaking to John.

"Why?"

"Because you have used magic."

John looked at Amy and shook his head. "That's not really true about me using magic," he said, turning back to Lisa Giles. "Something happened to me one time, and I don't even know what to call it."

Lisa Giles smiled, and again John found her calmness remarkable. "Call it whatever you wish. *We* would call what happened through you to be magic, and in fact it is our belief that you are one of the most powerful magic users on the planet."

John shook his head. "There's no way."

"No, John," Amy said, her voice firm. "I was there that night. I saw what you did in the catacombs, and I told Lisa. That's why she's come to speak with you."

Giles glanced at Amy then back to John. "We believe it's vital for you to learn to understand your gift and, if you can, to learn to control it."

"The point is I *can't* control it," John shot back.

"How do you know?" Lisa Giles insisted. "Do you have any idea what triggers magic and what it really is?"

John shook his head.

"Don't listen to her! Some things are not *meant* to be controlled," Faust shouted.

John turned to look at the priest. "Some things are triggered by the presence of evil," Faust went on. "Think about it! Your Putnam blood makes it possible for you to sense evil, just like a hunting dog can smell a pheasant."

John closed his eyes and shook his head and felt like Faust's words placed a terrible weight on his shoulders. He wanted to deny them, but he knew they were true. "What did you expect me to do?"

"To fight the Coven!" Faust shouted

"But if I have some kind of power, but I can't control it, what good am I going to be to anybody?"

Lisa Giles cleared her throat again. "Why don't you ask your friend, Father Faust, what was supposed to happen to you in this struggle against the Devil?"

John turned to Faust. "Well?"

Faust raised his chin, and his expression became cold. "If you are truly a magic user, as we also suspect, then in some part of your soul, whether you realize it or not, you are allied with the Devil."

John started to shake his head.

"Deny it all you want," Faust continued. "Mankind is not meant to use magic. It is the stuff of evil and ungodliness. Those who use magic are to be destroyed."

"So, if I had agreed to help you, I was supposed to die in the process?"

"You are a magic user."

"And you are a sick sonofabitch, Father Faust," John said.

"Now that you know he intended for you to die, what do you want to do with him?" Giles asked.

John looked at the small woman. Whatever it was about her that just moments ago had struck him as mousy and weak had disappeared, and she now seemed tough-minded and decisive, a woman accustomed to being in charge. "What do you mean by that?"

"If you let him go, he and his associates will try and kill you."

John turned and gazed at Faust for a long moment. The priest said nothing, and he took the man's silence as an indication that what Giles was saying was correct. Faust would indeed try to kill him; he would try to kill all of them. He glanced at Amy, who was still holding both knives and who looked as if she would instantly kill the priest if John gave the word.

"Would you really be stupid enough to try and kill me before I fight the Coven? If they're holding my daughter, it doesn't seem like I have any choice where that's concerned."

Still Faust refused to speak.

"So, what was your plan? You'd get me to attack the Coven and wait to see whether I won or got killed, and then you and your ODX friends would kill whoever survived? In other words, you saved my life yesterday only so you could make sure when I died I would do you good?"

Faust's mouth twitched, and a flicker of uncertainty seemed to pass across his face. Faust held his gaze but said nothing.

"Still," John went on, "no matter what your reasons, you did save my life, so in turn I'm going to save yours by letting you go. Get out of here. If I see you again, I'll do the same thing to you I did to the Coven leaders. I'm going to learn how to control that power, and I guarantee I'll use it on you."

"Think carefully," Giles began.

John cut her off. "I have."

CHAPTER TWENTY-FIVE

John kept the priest's gun and fished the silencer out of Faust's coat pocket, then he walked him to the front door. "One more thing, Faust," he said as he opened the door to let the priest walk out. "I'm saving your life by turning the other cheek the way the Bible says. Think carefully about that, Father Faust. Think about it before you try to kill me in God's name."

Faust looked at him, his expression a contest between anger and something else John couldn't name. He hoped he might see uncertainty or even shame, but he couldn't be sure. Finally, Faust gave an imperceptible nod, turned, and stepped out onto the sidewalk where he walked quickly away.

John came back into the house and found Lisa Giles and Amy back in the kitchen where Amy had poured them both mugs of hot coffee. He turned toward Amy. "Time for a little disclosure, perhaps?" he said in a sarcastic voice.

Amy nodded. "Okay."

John glanced at Giles then back to Amy. "Obviously, you two aren't strangers."

"No."

"When were you going to tell me you're a Wiccan? Or should I ask why you hadn't told me already?"

"I'm not a practicing Wiccan, but I've been interested in the religion for a long time."

"And you know this woman?" "Know Lisa Giles? Yes, very well." "And you told her to come here?"

"I had a suspicion that Faust wasn't telling us the whole truth."

John looked away from her, trying to control the anger and confusion and hurt he felt. "Why didn't you tell me she was coming ahead of time?"

"I didn't know how you'd react to a witch coming to the house. I thought you might suspect she was allied with the Satanists."

John nodded, privately admitting she was exactly right about his reaction. "Why shouldn't I still suspect that?"

Lisa Giles cleared her throat. "May I attempt to explain some things?"

John looked at her, realizing that the woman who had first shown up at his door had been trying to appear as less than she was. Now, she had dropped her guise of insubstantiality and appeared alert and in charge, very much like a woman who might be the CEO of a good-sized company. He was drawn to her and realized his instincts were to trust Lisa Giles. He went to the counter, poured himself a mug of coffee, and raised it to her in a salute. "Okay, your dime."

Lisa returned his gesture with a formal dip of her head. "Everything I told you a moment ago is true. We Wiccans use magic, at least we try to. We believe magic exists in our world, very much like an as-yet-undiscovered science. People outside the Wiccan religion believe magic is nonsense, or if it exists at all, it's inherently evil; however, their unbelief or dislike doesn't mean either is true.

"I would say the attitude toward magic today is a little bit like the church's attitude toward science back in the 1400s when their theology insisted the earth was flat and at the center of the universe. Church leaders feared to discover they might be wrong, and they persecuted those who claimed to know differently.

"So," she went on, "we Wiccans believe that magic exists, but we are the first to admit we are inexpert at manipulating it. The one thing we have is what you might call a heightened sensitivity to magic when it is near us, either in the outer world or in an individual. For example, in your case, I sense your magic," she paused and seemed to search for a word, "profoundly."

John looked at Amy to see her reaction, and she nodded, silently encouraging him not to reject what Lisa was saying.

Lisa went on. "If magic were sound, it's as if I have become accustomed to hearing very soft noises, but when you use magic, it's as if I'm hearing a sonic boom."

John started shaking his head. "That's where you're very wrong," he insisted. "I don't use magic. I don't know the first thing about it. I don't care about it, I don't study it, and I've never tried to use it."

"What do you call what you did the other night? That's what I'm talking about."

John glanced at Amy, who was nodding her encouragement, but he wasn't ready to go that far with his trust, not by a long shot. He turned back to Lisa. "I'm not sure what you mean."

"I'm talking about the magical equivalent of a twenty- thousand-pound bomb. Every witch in our coven has been walking around with a migraine headache since it happened."

John shrugged. "I really don't have a clue what you're referring to."

"Please trust me," Lisa insisted. "It's critical for all of us that do."

John looked at her and tried to calm his pulse. Every fiber of his being wanted to reject what she was saying. "Go on," he said.

"Every person, if they have any at all, has an aura that is as utterly unique as their DNA."

John still tried to shrug it off. "You're saying it was such a loud noise, you *could* be mistaken, right?"

Lisa shook her head. "I'm afraid not. It would be like turning up Frank Sinatra until it was so loud it made people's ears

bleed. It would be painful in the extreme, but there would be no mistaking that the voice was Sinatra's."

John took a long sip of coffee and saw that his hands were shaking. He glanced at Amy again. She nodded, clearly wanting him to open up to this woman. "So, let's say something did happen," he said. "What do you think it was? I just have to tell you before you answer that it wasn't *me* doing magic. It was . . . other entities."

Lisa smiled. "You don't think it was you because I'm sure you weren't trying to do anything other than survive and maybe save some lives."

"I wasn't doing magic," John insisted, his voice rising. "Something came into me."

Lisa held up her hands in a calming motion. "The only way another spirit could invest itself in you is when *you* allow that to happen. Most people are unaware of other spirits. They go through their whole lives never even sensing other presences around them."

"*You* have to understand something," John shot back. "I wasn't trying to sense anything. I hadn't ever sensed any spirits, but then Rebecca Nurse showed up aa week before Halloween."

"You'd *never* sensed another spirit?"

John screwed up his mouth, recalling the time years earlier when there had been a dorm fire, and something, a voice, had awakened him and saved his life and those of his roommates. "Maybe one other time," he admitted. "But it was years ago. Since then, I hadn't ever thought about spirits.

I certainly hadn't been thinking about letting Rebecca Nurse come into me, and I wasn't thinking about any of those other spirits, either." He finished his mug of coffee then grabbed the pot and poured more into all three mugs

"John," Amy said softly, "stop trying so hard to object. Lisa's trying to tell you that it's possible to do magic without even realizing it. We *know* you didn't try to do anything that night. That's the whole point."

John looked back and forth between them then pulled out a stool and sat heavily. For the second time that night he felt like he had a five-hundred-pound weight on his back. "What if I don't *want* to be magic."

"I'm afraid there's not much you can do about it. It's like wishing you weren't tall," Lisa said. "I will tell you that all the witches I know would kill to have your power."

"They can have it."

"No, they can't, and that's the point. That's why I came here. I need to make you believe me." Lisa's eyes tightened and she gave him a hard look. "Are you committed to fighting the Satanists?"

John nodded without needing to give it any thought. "Yes.

They have my daughter." Lisa nodded. "I know."

John glanced at Amy again, but she shook her head. "How do you know?"

"I felt it." She waited a second, but he didn't offer any objection. "Do you have any idea how you're going to fight them?"

John let out a heavy sigh. "No."

"I thought not. You need to prepare. Faust would have had you go straight over to England and confront Jessica Lodge, and that would have cost you your life."

John raised his eyebrows. "She's an old lady."

"Your eyes fool you. She's far, far more powerful than you could suspect. You need to prepare yourself to confront her."

"How? Do I need to do pushups?"

"John," Amy chided. "She's trying to help."

John shook his head. "Sorry. This stuff gets under my skin. How do I prepare?"

"You need to fly to Warsaw and from there to Kraków."

John looked at her in disbelief. "Poland?"

CHAPTER TWENTY-SIX

When Lisa Giles left the house, John walked her to the door and then watched as she made her way across the street to a parked car. Halfway expecting to see Father Faust jump out from behind a tree and start shooting, John was relieved to see that as Giles approached the car, she wasn't alone. Someone was behind the wheel, and as Lisa approached, they started the engine and the car pulled away from the curb to wait for her. Lisa climbed into the passenger seat, and the car with the unknown driver made a quick U-turn and drove away.

As John turned to go back inside, he felt he was being watched. He looked around the street at the empty sidewalk and the few cars parked along the curb, he could see no one. Finally, he gave a shrug, headed inside, and double-locked the door.

When he turned Amy was standing in the hallway behind him. He looked at her for a long time. Part of him was hurt and angry that she'd been holding back vital information, but the other part grudgingly understood.

"Truth time," he said. She nodded.

"Have you been with me because you really *wanted* to be with me, or have you been here because you're on some kind of undercover assignment for the Wiccans?"

Amy took a deep breath and let it out slowly before she started to answer. "That answer is complicated," she said. "I first came to the paper because I needed a job but also because a Wiccan friend called me and told me there was an opening at the paper."

John felt the world starting to crumble around him. "And they told you that because?" he asked, trying to keep voice from betraying the pain he felt.

"They were concerned you might need protection." "From the Coven?"

She nodded.

"And you would protect me how?"

"When I came to work for you, I told you I'd moved back East because I had gotten divorced and wanted a change of scenery."

"Yeah, that is what you said."

"Well, that part was true, but I also told you I'd been in the newspaper business. That part wasn't true. I had a friend supply you with a false employment history. I never worked for his paper."

John felt his face coloring as his anger started to surge. "So," he said, his voice a rasp, "who did you work for?"

"The FBI."

"You were an agent?" She nodded.

"Which is where you learned the knife trick?" She shrugged. "I improvised on that one." "Well, you improvised very well."

"And why did your friend go to so much trouble to give you a fake history? Was it your tremendous desire to learn the craft of journalism? Or was it something to do with becoming my babysitter?"

Amy closed her eyes and shook her head. "At first it seemed like a good thing to do because a group of people I respect thought you might need help."

John shook his head in disbelief. "Why didn't they just come to me?"

"Would you have believed Lisa if she'd come to your door? 'Hi, I'm a local Wiccan leader, and I'm here to tell you that the members of a group known as the Salem Coven are Devil worshipers and they've been running in Salem for over three hundred years. And oh, they killed your wife and will certainly make another attempt on your life because they fear you may have secret spiritual powers.'"

"But you've been working at the paper for years now.

What made you stick around?"

Amy gave him a bittersweet smile. "Two reasons. One, I really developed a liking for it." John waited. "And?" he said after a minute had gone by.

"And you, stupid. I wanted to be with you, and I didn't care about the assignment anymore. Well, I care about it because I want to keep you alive, but the assignment isn't why I'm here—not anymore." Amy ran her hands through her hair. "Look I'm sorry I didn't tell you any of this earlier, but I didn't know how to start the conversation. If you don't want to have any more to do with me, I understand."

John took all that in and let it settle. Finally, when he trusted his voice again, he nodded. "Well, it would be a shame to send you away so that you couldn't protect your little editor man."

Amy screwed up her face in a wry smile. "Do I have to remind you that when push came to shove, it was you who rescued me?"

John stepped toward her and took her in his arms. "You know as well as I do, I wasn't trying to be some kind of hero that night. I just wanted to get you out of there and make sure you were okay."

"You came down into the catacombs to find me. Most people would call that heroic, but you can call it whatever you want."

John smiled, but then his smile disappeared, and he became coldly serious. "You've got to understand this magic stuff is hard for me to deal with. I don't want any part of it."

Amy ran a hand through his hair and used a thumb to smooth his wrinkled brow. "I know, but it may be the only thing that will help you get Sarah back." "You really believe that don't you?" She nodded.

He took a deep breath and tried to steel himself for what he had to do. "Okay," he said after Let's get going. We need to get into work. We have one paper to bury and another one to birth, and I have to write my farewell editorial."

"We also need to make some airline reservations." "We?"

"I'm coming with you."

CHAPTER TWENTY-SEVEN

The rest of the day at the paper was exhausting and emotionally difficult, but for John the positive aspect was it allowed him to forget about Sarah's abduction, the Salem Coven, Jessica Lodge, and Father Faust. He spent the afternoon writing his farewell editorial, in which he recounted the events that had shaped the city of Salem over the years he'd served as executive editor.

He also took the opportunity to inform his readers of the launching of the *Salem Observer*, telling them that everyone who was a subscriber to the *Salem News* would receive a free two-week subscription to the new paper beginning Monday. With his part of the final edition put to bed, John went out into the newsroom to meet with Amy, Jack, Lucinda,

Jackie, and Tim to make sure that they had everything lined up for Monday's edition. Lucinda assured him the delivery people were all lined up to make sure that the new paper would be on the exact same doorsteps the *Salem News* had been going to.

Amy had copied all the subscription records so that names and addresses were all in a computer file that would be transferred to the new paper. Jackie McKinney said the first week's ad sales had been extremely encouraging. Every business in town saw the value in a local daily paper and wanted to help support the effort. Amy also explained how the new printing contract worked and how and at what time the electronic files needed to be over to assure prompt response.

Jack Daniels gave John a rueful smile and shook his head. "I can't believe we're doing this. I mean, I can't believe I'm leaving money on the table and signing up to work for an incompetent son of a bitch editor like you."

"I certainly feel the same about you," John said. "It's hard to find somebody whose dependability is so low you're actually surprised when they show up for work."

Jack smiled happily. "I always bring that elusive *je ne sais quoi* to every situation."

"Is *je ne sais quoi* what you call a bucket full of crap in Ireland?" Hagstrom grumbled.

"His parents didn't have any money, so that's what they fed him for dinner every night when he was a kid," Monahan added. "He can't help himself. Bullshit is his core. If the doc-

tors cut him open, that's all they'd find."

"And a very high-quality load of bullshit it would be, I tell you, "Said Daniels.

"The other thing I've got to tell you is you're going to have to get the paper off the ground without me. We're going over- seas tomorrow. I don't know how long we'll be gone."

"Amy's going with you?" Lucinda Jenkins asked.

Was John wrong or did he see the beginning of a smile at the corners of Lucinda's mouth? Feeling his cheeks start to redden, he said, "Yes," in as brusque a voice as he could manage.

"Don't mean to pry," Jackie McKinney said in a gentle voice, "but does this relate to Sarah in any way?"

John hesitated, and then he nodded. "I hope so."

"We wish you luck, and don't worry about the paper.

We'll get it out just fine."

"Actually, without you around to screw things up, we'll probably win a Pulitzer," Jack Daniels said.

"Thanks for the good thoughts, Jack. I hope you don't fall and break a leg on your way to the bar."

Jack smiled. "Liquor makes the joints extra loose. We may fall, but we don't hurt ourselves."

Lucinda groaned. "I can't take any more. I'm going back to work."

"A first for the week," Jack said.

"I'll get the first couple editorials written today before I leave," John offered. "And I can send others in electronically, if necessary."

"Don't worry about the paper," Hagstrom assured him.

"We'll get it out, and we'll keep Daniels in line."

John stood up and walked back into his office, grateful for the distraction from all his other troubles. He wrote four editorials, the first one outlining the new *Salem Observer's* goals and how they'd be like the defunct *Salem News*. The next three editorials dealt with the importance of a daily newspaper to the fabric of a community; the importance of printing the truth about the community, even though that truth was sometimes unpleasant or hard to swallow; and finally one that talked about the nine people who comprised the new owners and staff of the *Salem Observer*, giving special visibility to the people who at any paper were normally invisible, the people without mastheads, namely Lucinda, Tim, and Bert.

Finally, he made reservations for himself and Amy on the next evening's Lufthansa flight from Boston to Warsaw, Poland, with a stop in Munich. From Warsaw they would connect to the fifty-minute flight to Kraków on LOT. He waved to Amy through the glass walls of his office and when she stepped inside, he showed her the reservation.

"What do we do when we get to Kraków?" he asked. "I'll call Lisa and tell her what we're doing and get instructions."

"Instructions?" John repeated, bridling. "I'll work *with*

Lisa Giles, but I won't take orders from her."

Amy left the office and came back a few moments later. "Lisa suggests you make a reservation at the Hotel Wentzl in Kraków, and someone will contact us."

John closed his eyes and shook his head. "Are you sure this makes sense?"

Amy nodded. "I really am."

"Okay," John grumbled as he turned back to his computer. "I'll make the reservation."

Shortly after he finished making the reservation, he received a phone call from Chester Cabot, Jessica Lodge's lawyer. "Mr. Andrews," Cabot began. "I just wanted to make sure you and your staff would vacate the newspaper offices no later than five thirty this evening. At that point, the doors will be locked, and any personal belongings left in the newspaper offices will be forfeit."

"We'll leave tonight when we're good and ready," John shot back. "And if you or any of your goons come in here and try to lock the place before everyone has gotten their stuff out in their own good time, I will personally separate your balls from your scrawny body. Do we understand each other, Cabot?"

"Five thirty, Andrews. Don't push it." Chester Cabot hung up.

By five o'clock that afternoon, they had the final edition of the paper put to bed, and John had finished polishing his first four editorials for the new paper in addition to his farewell for the *Salem News*. Out in the newsroom, the atmosphere was getting emotional as people finished packing up their personal items and getting ready to leave for the last time. Several people, including Lucinda, were dabbing their eyes with tissues as they hugged and reminisced with the others on the staff about all the years they had worked together.

The nine people who would make up the initial staff of the *Salem Observer* were all moving with greater purpose because they all knew what they were going to be doing on Monday morning, but the other thirty-three employees of the old *Salem News* stood in small groups, looking lost and forlorn. John had finished packing up his desk. He walked out of his office at exactly five after five and called out, "My final order is that every single person report to The Old Spot as soon as you carry your stuff out to your car."

He waited as everyone carried boxes of photos and note-pads and whatever else to their cars. He and Amy did the same thing, taking their boxes to his car. Afterward, every-one returned to the newsroom and stood in a group looking at him. He could see the tears in almost every eye as he made eye contact with each person. John looked around, taking in the walls, the silence, and the sadness of the empty desks. He opened his mouth, intending to tell them how proud he was of each person who'd worked for the paper, how they'd each done an outstanding job, and how as a team they'd combined their strengths to put out a truly excellent paper, day after day, year after year.

He tried to get the words out but felt his throat close. He took three slow breaths, trying each time to get control, and finally all he could croak out was, "Let's go get a drink."

They walked out of the offices in a solitary group. John went last. He cleaned out the petty cash drawer and stuffed the money in his pocket, and then, not bothering to turn off the lights or lock the door, he left. He was sure Chester Cabot would be there not a second later than five thirty to lock it for him. If Cabot didn't show up and the place got robbed or burned down, he couldn't have cared less.

CHAPTER TWENTY-EIGHT

T he old spot was crowded, and when people heard why, the entire staff of the paper had come *en masse*, and others started showing up, buying drinks for the staff, one round after another. Predictably, Jack Daniels led the group onward, drinking more than anyone else and loudly declaiming they were there to take part in a wake, mourning the death of the *Salem News*. The group, joined by others in the bar and friends who wandered in to join them, went ahead to lurch between tears and hilarity as they told war stories about their years working at the *Salem News*.

When he had finally drunk himself into a fair state of inebriation, Daniels raised his glass at the start of a fresh round and in a sonorous voice said, "May Jessica Lodge's saggy old tits rot off in hell."

People hesitated for a moment, and then they all raised their glasses. "Here, here," they chorused.

Warmed by one round of drinks after another, John looked around at his old staff as he raised his glass, wondering how many of them could be members of the Coven. Was it one or two? More? Had Jack Daniels just put his own life in dan- ger by making that toast? John shook his head, hating the paranoia and suspicion that were increasingly guiding his perception of the people around him, but hating even more the knowledge that the people of Salem had held deep and evil secrets for over three hundred years and that those secrets had managed to remain buried.

If people like his great-great-grandfather Captain John Bancroft Andrews and Nathaniel Hawthorne had been frightened enough to silence their criticism of the Coven during their lifetimes, he knew the Coven had a power and a reach he should never underestimate. But the fact was he had underestimated both their reach and their determination to protect their own, and as a result they had abducted his daughter.

And now he was about to fly out of the country to find out just how far the Coven's tentacles extended through the world and to "prepare" himself to face Jessica Lodge—what- ever the hell that meant—to try to get Sarah back safely. He shook his head, feeling a sudden surge of anger that he had no goddamn idea what he was supposed to do when he got to Kraków, and he didn't know a thing about the person who was supposed to meet them. And he was doing all of this at whose recommendation: a freaking Wiccan? What was he thinking?

Jack Daniels snapped him out of his angry reverie when he came over and put a huge arm around John's shoulders. "Another toast," Daniels intoned, "to the worst enemy of tangled syntax, inaccurate modifiers, excessive adjectives, and inexactitude of every nature. To a man who hates adverbs the way exterminators hate rats. To a man who sat in the glass office boxing our ears when we were naughty and staring us into submission when we were truculent. To a man whose fairness and courage I cannot dispute, as much as I would like to, because a good Irishman always disputes everything." He squeezed John's shoulders hard and emptied a shot of Bushmills down his throat as the others all cheered and followed suit with whatever they were drinking.

John had been trying to keep himself sober through the endless chain of toasts, but he realized he was succeeding only to a degree. Suddenly hit by realization that members of his staff were quite drunk and feeling responsible that no one was killed or arrested on their way home, he grabbed the bartender and told him to take the car keys from anyone who seemed too drunk to drive. John said he would pay for taxis for anyone who needed one, and he counted out six hundred dollars of the money he had taken from petty cash and handed it across the bar.

"That's for the drinks, however many taxis you need to call, and the rest is for you. If it's not enough, let me know and I'll make you good."

John held up a glass and dinged a knife against the side until he got a reasonable amount of silence. "I toast all of you," he said, the liquor in his system giving him the ability to get the words out without choking up. "You have been the best staff. It's been an honor. I will you on Monday morning, and to the rest of you I wish you all the best luck in the world. If any of you want to come back into the newspaper business after your non-compete has run out, you know where to find us. Good night, good luck, and be safe." A cheer went up from the others in the bar, but then, as John and Amy got ready to leave, Jackie, Tim, and Bert all

came up to him. "We'll walk you home," Hagstrom said.

Surprised, John looked back and forth between them. "That's not necessary."

"Your daughter's missing. We talked it over among our-selves, and we just want to make sure nothing happens to you."

John hesitated, glancing at Amy. They had been trying to keep their new relationship a secret, although something told him that they had not succeeded at all. Amy smiled and shrugged, and John nodded. "Okay, thanks."

They walked in silence the few short blocks back to John's house on Pickering Wharf. When they reached his front door, John turned to face his friends and say goodnight, and Amy came to stand beside him, taking his arm and thereby leaving no trace of doubt in anyone's mind as to the nature of their relationship.

"Thanks again, guys," John said, and the smiles he got back told him that they were pleased for more than just seeing him safely home.

Thirty minutes later John was in bed, while Amy was in the bathroom getting ready. John heard the door open and looked up to find Amy walking to him naked. Her legs were long and lean, her hips just wide enough to be feminine, and her breasts full and high with the nipples erect with the chill.

It took a moment and then he found his voice. "Wow," he managed. "You are so out of my league. God, you're beautiful."

Amy crossed the room and climbed into bed. She turned on her side and looked at him. "I know you were taken by surprise when Lisa came to the house, and once again, I'm sorry about that."

"Don't worry about it," John mumbled, no longer caring about Lisa Giles or Father Faust or Jessica Lodge and for a few blessed moments, even Sarah.

"How much do you know about witchcraft?" Amy asked John blinked, surprised by that question, and not caring in the least whether he knew anything at all about witchcraft at

that moment. "Not much." "Have you ever heard of the Great Rite?"

"No. Does it have something to do with beautiful naked women?"

"As a matter of fact, yes." "Then I think I'd like to learn."

"Good answer. The Great Rite is where the High Priest and the High Priestess invoke the God and Goddess by per- forming sexual intercourse to raise the magical energy that used in their spell work."

"Are you being straight with me?" "Yes."

"I don't know why I haven't been a Wiccan all my life." "Well, it's usually performed symbolically where athame is used to represent the penis and a chalice is used to represent the womb."

"An athame?"

"A ritual dagger or knife." "Are we going to be symbolic?"

"No. I'm afraid I don't have a ritual dagger. Do you have one?"

"I'm afraid not."

"Well, since neither of us has a ritual dagger, we'll have to use the real thing. "

"I see."

"Do you approve?" "Very definitely."

"Then get out of your pajamas and let the High Priestess show you what you need to do."

"Yes, ma'am."

CHAPTER TWENTY-NINE

The following morning Amy eagerly accepted John's suggestion they practice the Great Rite once again. In his words, "We just need to make sure we get it right," they met Lisa Giles for breakfast at Maria's Place. Lisa had arrived ahead of them, and as John and Amy walked into the small restaurant, Lisa watched them and came to a conclusion about what might have taken place the night before, because she was smiling warmly by the time, they reached the table and sat.

John felt his face coloring, and he sought refuge behind a menu as he pretended to think about what he wanted for breakfast. When the server came over, he waited for Lisa and Amy to order then he ordered coffee, juice, and two eggs over easy with whole wheat toast and crisp bacon. He realized he not only had an appetite for the first time in a while. He was famished.

He felt different and more alive in more ways than just his rediscovered appetite and knew his and Amy's version of the Great Rite had been just what the doctor ordered. And a second later he suffered a strong blast of guilt as he realized everything that had happened over the past twenty-four hours had sidetracked him badly from the task of finding and rescuing Sarah.

Lisa interrupted his jumbled thoughts by saying, "Yesterday, I told you about myself. I hope you have had enough time to get comfortable with the fact that we are on the same side in this struggle, and that I will do every- thing in my power to see you are successful in overcoming Jessica Lodge and getting your daughter home safely. I hope you will trust me enough to tell me exactly what has happened to you over the past couple of days.

Amy has shared a small amount, but it would be extremely helpful to hear it from your perspective."

John glanced at Amy, who gave a nearly imperceptible nod, and after a second he leaned across the table and in a low voice told her everything had happened since Sarah's abduction, including his discovery that the police captain who appeared to be his friend, Andrew Card, had not been a policeman after all, but a member of ODX, and how John had found Card's horribly tortured body in a secret room at the top of the House of the Seven Gables. He also told Lisa about the two people who had tried to kill him in the parking

lot at the House of the Seven Gables and how Father Faust had killed them and then left their bodies in the trunk of their car at Logan Airport."

Lisa listened without interrupting, and when John finished, she folded her hands on her placemat and bowed her head in deep contemplation.

John cleared his throat after a time. "I have to tell you, all things being equal, my highest priority is finding my daughter and getting her back here in one piece."

Lisa raised her eyes, which were piercing and as grey as a winter sky. "Your daughter is alive," she said without the slightest hesitation, "but she is in great danger."

"Then I've got to get to England. I don't have time for a detour to Poland."

Lisa's eyes tightened. "If you go to England today, you will be dead tomorrow. I guarantee it. So will Amy. If you don't care about yourself, at least give some thought to her welfare."

John glared back. "Then tell me what I'm supposed to do when I get to Kraków."

"Wait for someone to contact you."

"Another witch?" John said in a mocking tone. "No."

John glared at Lisa Giles, but she gave him the glare right back. "You need to trust me, Mr. Andrews. Everything depends on you doing that."

CHAPTER THIRTY

The next day before they left John and Amy took all the precautions they could. John checked his Audi, both under the rear fender and inside the engine compartment, just the way Father Faust had done two days earlier. Then before carrying their suitcases out to the car, he had Amy go out and check the street to make sure it was empty. On the way to the airport, they took an indirect route, doubling back to make certain they weren't followed.

Not knowing how long they would be gone, they put the car in long-term parking and went to the terminal, looking around constantly to see if there was any sign of a tail. The flight itself was on time, and it was long and uneventful. John managed a couple hours of disjointed sleep on the way, and they landed in Kraków at four p.m. Poland time a day later.

Following Lisa's instructions, they went to the Hotel Wentzl, checked in, ate dinner in the hotel dining room, and went to bed. John was pleased they were able to reenact the Great Rite yet again, and afterwards as he lay in the dark with Amy's head on his chest, listening to her breathe, he wondered if making love could have helped prepare them in any way for what followed. He had no idea if it could really be true, but he hoped that in addition to leaving him feeling wonderful, it was.

They awoke the next morning before the sun was even up, and having nothing better to do, they enacted the Great Rite yet again. "I think I'm developing a greater and greater respect for the Wiccan religion," John noted when they were lying together in the sleepy aftermath.

"I think you're developing a greater and greater respect for acting like a randy teenager."

"It's all your fault." "I sincerely hope so."

They went downstairs around seven and were drinking coffee and munching freshly baked rolls when the maître d' came to their table. "Excuse, please. A man is asking for you. Should I send him to your table?"

John glanced toward the door and saw a man in a black suit with a long dark beard. He felt a twinge of alarm, wondering if this was indeed the person Lisa Giles had sent or if it might be an imposter sent by the Coven. He glanced at Amy, who nodded her assent, and despite his misgivings, he nodded as well. "Please," he told the man.

A moment later the bearded man approached their table. As he got closer John could see the man was younger than he'd first guessed, maybe not even thirty, but his face seems older by the thick beard. At first John had thought the man looked thickly built, even heavy, but as he came toward them John could see he was thin with narrow shoulders and long arms that initially looked larger because the of very full cut of his dark clothes. Also, John now saw the yarmulke on the back of the man's head.

The man came to a stop and eyed them both, his eyes watery with what looked like exhaustion and suspicion. "John Andrews?" he asked, looking at John. "And Amy Johnson?" he said as he turned his eyes on Amy.

"Yes," they both answered. "May I sit?"

"Who told you to find us?" John asked.

"A woman in the United States named Lisa Giles," the man said, his English excellent but spoken with a British accent.

John reached over and pulled out a chair. "Have a seat."

The man sat, folded his hands on the table, and waited while the waiter put a napkin and silverware in front of him and poured coffee into his cup. When the waiter finished and walked away, the man leaned into the center of the table and said in faint voice, "I am Rabbi Pawel Czarnecki, and I have been asked to spend the day with you. Pretend I am your tour guide," he said with a smile.

"No offense, Rabbi, but I don't have time to screw around on a tour," John said.

"Neither do I, but to anyone observing us we need to make it look like a tour, understand?"

"Yes," Amy said very softly, then louder, "great I'm excited."

The rabbi turned to John. "Please play along," he whispered.

"Okay," John said, loud enough for anyone in the dining room to overhear, "let's get going."

They finished their coffee, John signed the check, and then they walked out of the hotel onto Kraków's main market square. The day was cool with a blustery wind, and they each pulled on overcoats and buttoned them tight to their throats as they followed the rabbi to the right where they followed a road called Grodzka away from the square and through an old part of the city.

They walked ten or fifteen minutes past the Uniwersytet Papieski Jana Pawla II, a six-hundred-year-old Catholic university on the left side of the street, and a large church on the right that Czarnecki said was St. Andrew's Church. They came at last to a large intersection and Czarnecki pointed to the right where a large castle rose above the buildings around it.

"Wawel Castle was begun sometime between 1330 and 1370 by Casimir III the Great," he said as he crossed the street toward the castle walls. He told them a bit about the castle as they walked, but John was hardly listening because two separate times he caught Czarnecki exchanging glances with people on the street. One had appeared to be a shopkeeper who had been sweeping the sidewalk in front of his small shop, and the other appeared to be one of the guards outside the castle itself after they walked through a broad entrance into the center part of the castle and were walking out the other side.

"Who are those people?" John asked after the second man gave Czarnecki a nod that was more than casual.

"They are making sure we're not being followed." "And?"

"For now, we are clear."

Outside the castle again, they crossed the road and went to a small car park where Czarnecki led them to a well-used Peugeot sedan. John climbed into the front passenger seat and Amy got into the rear and they drove off with a broad river glittering off to their left.

They moved from the old section of the city to newer sections with taller, more modern buildings and quickly got on a four-lane limited access highway that swept them out of the city. Czarnecki said little as he drove, just looked in the rearview mirror every few seconds as if he was continuing to watch for tails.

"Where are we going?" John asked after the long silence began to grate on his nerves.

"Gmina Oswiecim," Czarnecki said. John shook his head. "Why?"

"Lisa Giles instructed me to bring you here."

"You know she's a witch, right?" John asked. "You're a rabbi, and you're doing what she tells you?"

Czernecki gave him a questioning glance. "Yes."

"Do you have any idea why she wants you to bring me here?"

Again, a glance, but this time it was hooded, as if Czarnecki was only going to share a certain amount of information. "I have a guess."

"You want to share it?"

"No."

CHAPTER THIRTY-ONE

As Sarah came down the long staircase to the bottom floor of the house, she could see muted morning light coming in through the tall windows in the parlor to her right. To her left, in the dining room, she spotted Jessica Lodge already at the table with her cup of hot tea to one side and the morning papers spread out before her on the table. At the sound of Sarah's footsteps, Jessica looked up and smiled.

"Good morning, my dear. Are you well rested?"

Sarah nodded. "Yes, very, thank you." Over the past however many days—she had lost count somewhere along the way—she had come to feel like a favorite granddaughter making an extended visit in her grandmother's large house.

"Well, sit down and have some breakfast, and we can decide where we should walk this morning."

Sarah pulled out a chair and sat down. Jessica picked up a small glass bell and rang it for the house cleaner. A second later a woman in a black uniform with starched white cuffs and a white apron bustled through the swinging door that led to the kitchen.

"Breakfast, madam?" the house cleaner asked.

"Yes," Sarah said. "Tea and juice please, and a couple of scrambled eggs."

"Sausage and toast, madam?"

"Why not?" Sarah said with a small laugh. "I might as well make myself fat."

The house cleaner nodded and disappeared, and Jessica looked up from her paper again. "It's a bit colder this morning. You'll want something warmer than just a Barbour coat. I'll get you a nice heavy sweater, pair of gloves, and a woolen cap for our walk."

Sarah smiled and nodded her thanks. Their walks had become part of the daily ritual, something that happened every morning without fail, whether it was raining or fair. Sarah was aware the walks had become gradually longer every day, and she realized that every day her body felt a little less heavy and that she felt capable of managing the added distance. Part of her brain recorded the fact that she'd been drugged ever since she had first awoken in this house, and she knew the drug dosages she was being given were declining every day. She was positive that was the reason she was capable of walking longer each morning.

The other things about the walks that struck her as unusual were twofold. First, Jessica Lodge was, according to Sarah's best guess, somewhere in her mid-eighties, but she seemed to move like a well-conditioned woman in her late fifties or early sixties. Her walking pace was brisk, she never stopped to catch her breath, and her flexibility and strength were that of a much younger person. There had been no day so far when Sarah hadn't been certain that Jessica could have walked her into the ground.

The second unusual thing about the walks wasn't just the fact that Jessica spoke almost nonstop from the time they left the house to the time they returned; it was the way Sarah heard two conversations at once. She heard the words Jessica spoke, but then underneath those words, like a television playing softly in the next room, she heard the undertone of a different conversation running on a parallel track so that when Jessica stopped talking the other conversation stopped as well. Sarah had ascribed it to one more effect from the drugs, but in a small part of her brain she wondered if it could be something else.

The house cleaner interrupted Sarah's thoughts as she came back into the room with a pot of fresh tea and glass of juice. She poured tea into Sarah's cup and put down the juice. When she went over to pour more tea into Jessica's cup, Sarah stole a glance at the newspaper, trying to see the day's date along the top of the page.

She had only made it as far as seeing the word November before Jessica moved the paper so that Sarah could no longer see it. For half a second Sarah felt a twinge of alarm. Had Jessica done that on purpose? Why didn't she want Sarah to see the paper? How long had she been here? Had it been October or November when she arrived?

"Jessica, could I see the paper?" she asked.

Jessica looked at her, and Sarah felt something coldly appraising in her glance before Jessica broke into another of her trademark smiles. "My dear, it was rude of me to be reading at the table. We are both here in this lovely place so we can rest up and regain our strength. A newspaper only pulls us back into the problems of the larger world and works against our recovery.

"What am I recovering from? I don't remember. I don't remember much of anything, in fact."

"Things were very traumatic back in Salem before you left. And then you were abducted, do you remember that?"

Sarah paused, trying to reassemble the memories. She had been getting out of her car when someone had grabbed her, she recalled that much. There had been a strange smell and then darkness, and then she'd awakened to find herself here. Finally, she shook her head. "No."

"Well, suffice it to say, you *were* abducted, but then we rescued you, and you've been recovering here ever since."

Sarah closed her eyes. Was that a different explanation than Jessica had previously given her? She wasn't sure, but she thought it might be. The problem was her brain was still so fuzzy she couldn't be certain of anything.

A moment later the house cleaner brought her breakfast, and the smell of freshly scrambled eggs, buttered toast, and sausage hit her nose and made her stomach rumble with hunger pangs. She forgot about her questions and whatever it was that had alarmed her and took a bite.

She succumbed to eating and enjoying the wonderful flavors of the food. Suddenly, sensual pleasures like eating, the feel of a hot bath on her skin when she lay in the tub every afternoon, or the warmth of crisp sheets when she lay under the comforter at night, all seemed more important to her than they ever had before. Even the pleasure of walking through the pastures and up the meandering country roads with Jessica, the smell of salt-laden air in her nostrils, and the tingle of clean wind on her cheeks had deeper meanings she had never been aware of before.

She had discovered the importance of feeling good of pleasing her senses, and she couldn't believe she had over emphasized her job for so many years and ignored her physical needs. In addition to the purely personal, she was starting to realize there was one other thing she wanted that she had ignored for just as long: a relationship.

Her good looks, inherited from her mother, had meant she'd always had opportunities for male companionship, but she had kept men at arm's length, believing that in any relationship the woman always ended up making more compromises than the man. Not wanting to be the one who had to make the inevitable career compromises, she had simply avoided entanglements in the first place. Now, however, along with wanting her skin soft and warm from a bath and her stomach full of healthy food and her muscles feeling toned and fresh from a good walk, she found herself missing another body beside her in bed, someone to speak to across the dinner table, someone in whom she could confide her innermost secrets.

"What are you thinking about, my dear?" Jessica asked, sounding friendly and interested, always concerned for Sar- ah's best interests.

Sarah paused, smiling before she answered. "I was thinking about having a man in my life," she said, thinking Jessica asked such penetrating questions but never seemed to be prying.

Jessica dabbed her lips with her napkin and stood up from the table. "Are you ready for your walk, my dear? You'll have to tell me all about this new interest of yours."

CHAPTER THIRTY-TWO

John sat in the front seat of the old Peugeot looking out the window as suburbs gave way to small farms and the countryside became hillier. Leaving Kraków, they climbed away from the valley around the Vistula River and drove through miles of farmland, the road sometimes winding back down into the valley to cut through a small town before heading back into the hills again. Finally, the road settled back into the valley, and they continued through an endless topography of farms until they came to an intersection and John saw the first sign for Oswiecim.

"Is that where we're going?" he asked.

Czarnecki nodded. They drove into the city of Oswiecim and out the other side, and they hadn't gone another mile before John felt his throat start to tighten up. He suddenly felt feverish, and his muscles began to tighten, his hands clenching and unclenching involuntarily.

He had seen people have allergic reactions to peanuts, and even though he wasn't allergic, he felt his airway begging to close off, and then a sound that started off as a soft wailing became stronger and stronger. John could see Czarnecki turning his head slightly and giving him a sideways glance. Czarnecki realized that whatever was happening to him was quite terrible, but he seemed to have expected it to happen because the rabbi did not slow the car.

John's first panicked thought was that the rabbi must be another Coven member who had figured out a way to poison him somehow. He tried to turn his head to see if Amy was having the same problem, but by this time he could barely move. The wailing sound had grown louder and louder and was now drowning out every other sound.

He tried to say something, tell Amy he needed help, but all he could manage was choking grunts. There was a touch on his shoulders and neck, a soothing, gentle touch, Amy's hands trying to tell him everything would be okay.

The car came to a halt. Up ahead he saw a building, austere and ugly and made of reddish-brown brick. The road seemed to dead end at the building, and to John life itself also seemed to end at the building. He felt so much pain, unimaginable pain, and by now the wailing had grown so loud he thought his ears must have been bleeding.

Things were deteriorating, his eyes tearing so badly he could barely see, his nose running, a mixture of snot and tears pouring down over his lips, his muscles cramping uncontrollably. He thought he was going to suffocate, that his mind was going to snap from the torture of the wails, and then, just when he thought he couldn't take it a second longer, it started to change.

He didn't know if the car was moving, but the wailing began to recede, and gradually his muscles loosened and breath came back into his lungs, just a fraction at first and then a bit more. He was aware of the car door opening and felt something soft on his face, and he realized Amy was cleaning him up and then pulling him to his feet.

Walking like an old man, he shuffled between Amy and Czarnecki, who held his arms as they walked toward the red brick building. They passed signs that he was unable to read, but he had the impression they were in a public place. The wailing continued to drop in volume and his muscles unclenched a bit more. When his breath had become more normal and he thought he could trust his voice, he asked, "Can you hear that?"

Amy looked at him, "Only when I touch you. If I let go, I can't hear it. Is it terrible?"

"Not as bad now as before."

"I still can't see very well. Where are we?"

"Just keep walking," Czarnecki said. "I think it will all become clear in a moment."

Czarnecki led them up to the very front of the building, and as they stepped close John suddenly saw and felt, and it was enough to take him to his knees. On both side of him there were suddenly vast numbers of people standing in a line. There were people, old and young; there were children and teenagers and infants in their mother's arms.

It wasn't just the people; it was what he felt, as if he were experiencing the totality of all their emotions all at the same time. He experienced rage and fear and terror and helplessness and unspeakable sorrow, each emotion totally outsized and all encompassing, something larger and more profound than a human being was meant to feel. As if the emotions were knives, John felt he was being cut to pieces and reassembled. As if they were stretching machines, he felt himself being pulled and wrenched as they were shoved inside of him with a pain that was so intense it crossed from being mental to being physical as well.

He felt his heart pounding, his blood pressure rising like an engine revving past the red line, and his nerve endings seeming to fragment under the load. When he looked down, he saw he was holding the hands of the nearest people on both sides, but he didn't know when he'd grasped them or how long he'd been holding them. The two on either side of him were old men, wearing black coats and black fedoras like Rabbi Charnecki's. Both men were silent and expectant, and they were looking at John with quiet intensity. The two men held out their other hands and people took them, as one by one all the people began to clasp hands until they were joined together in a chain that seemed to extend out a long, long way in either direction.

As John watched the line continued to grow, and he realized those people who had not yet become part of the hand-holding chain were wailing, but each time one of them joined their hand to the last person in line, they would fall silent and turn their silent gaze down the line toward John.

No one had told him what this place was called or who these people were, but he now understood at a level beyond the reach of words. He looked from side to side at the wide, expectant eyes and felt an anger begin to build inside him. Unlike the night in the catacombs beneath Salem, this anger was neither white hot nor uncontrollable. Nonetheless it was consuming, but more like the molten core of a star that might burn for eons rather than the quick, hot flash from a can of gasoline. John looked to either side, took in what had grown to be thousands of people standing hand in hand, a link of bodies that stretched to the horizon. He understood why he was here and what together they were supposed to conduct, and he nodded once in each direction.

Then he let go of the hands and turned to Czarnecki. "We can go now," he said, hearing only the sound of the cold

wind blowing across the lonely ground.

CHAPTER
THIRTY-THREE

As they drove away john turned in his seat and looked back at the austere building set in the middle of nowhere with bucolic farm fields on either side and the ruins of what must have been the dormitories of the prisoners before they were put to death behind. He turned back around and shuddered; his eyes not focused on anything. He felt like a man who had just had the crap pounded out of him in a bar fight so totally and completely that he was stunned into silence and submission. Amy's hands were on his shoulders, seeming to ground him into his existence.

The past few minutes were still a total blur. He had only stood there, probably not longer than five minutes, but looking back, it seemed like an eternity.

"Why didn't you tell me?" he asked, feeling the anger and resentment build.

"Tell you what?" Czarnecki asked.

"Where we were going. What was going to happen when we got there."

"Would you have come if we had?" Czarnecki asked.

John thought about the horror he had experienced. "I don't know."

He fell silent for a time, feeling Amy's fingers as they tried to massage the tightness from his muscles. "What am I sup- posed to do with it?" he asked after another long silence.

Czarnecki turned his head to look at him. "Doesn't it give you power of some kind?"

"I've no idea." John shook his head. "It's not something I can just call up, like a magic trick." He felt a hollowness inside, as if rather than filling him up, the spirits he had seen and experienced had exposed his glaring weakness and inadequacy.

"What do we do next, fly to London?" he asked, thinking about Sarah, and wondering whether what he'd just experienced would make even the slightest difference in helping to get her back safely.

"I need to call Lisa Giles and several others," Czarnecki said. "We need to share the information about what just happened. We hope you will agree to consult with us."

John looked straight ahead. "I didn't think Jews believed in witchcraft. Why are you following the dictates of a self- styled witch?"

Czarnecki took a deep breath and let it out slowly. "I'm not following anyone's dictates, Mr. Andrews. I'm a man of God. I believe in some things more than anything else. First, humans are profoundly imperfect and can convince themselves they have far more understanding than they really do. Second, I believe what I choose to call God is responsible for creation. What I see as Yahweh, the Wiccans see as multiple gods. Buddhists see the divine spirit as discoverable from profound internal contemplation. The Hindus see a pantheon of gods. Does that mean any of us are right? Of course not.

"I don't believe God is petty or mean-spirited. God doesn't care if I eat shellfish or pork, whether a Muslim gets on his knees to pray five times each day, or whether a Christian takes Jesus as his or her savior. Men created these differences in their attempts to dominate others through the ritualized practice of one particular form of worship. I believe only in the fact that God is creation and therefore the freedom of the human spirit to grow, learn, evolve, and explore, and the Devil represents the opposite—destruction, enslavement, and desecration. The struggle between the two is profound and eternal, but it is at a higher pitch today than at most other times in history."

John turned to look at the rabbi, surprised by what he had just heard. "Why now?" he asked.

"The rise of fundamentalism that makes people turn their back on science, deny evolution, and makes them see blind rituals and seek the destruction of those who worship differently. Does that sound like the worship of creation or the unknowing worship of destruction?"

You're saying that fundamentalism of all stripes is the product of the worshippers of the Devil?"

Czarnecki nodded. "Therefore, to answer your first question, yes, I willingly cooperate with a witch because I am confident that while she worships differently, she worships the same spirit of creation that I do."

John sat back and looked out the window and tried to reconcile what he was feeling inside with what the rabbi had just told him. He knew without being told that to Czarnecki and Giles and their other allies he stood for a defense against the powers of entropy and destruction. "I think the bad guys have the upper hand," he said.

"Sometimes they do, but they didn't this morning." "You think we actually accomplished something?" "When the wailing stopped, I think it was a sign." "A sign of what?"

"Of purpose." Czarnecki was still looking in the rearview mirror every few seconds. "I think one other thing, as well. I think the Coven knows what you just did."

CHAPTER THIRTY-FOUR

That morning Sarah awoke to the sound of a door slamming somewhere in the downstairs of the house. She could tell from the heaviness of the sound that it had to have been the thick front door with the big brass knocker in the shape of a demon's head. Next came the sound of footsteps clomping across the bare wooden floor, followed by the sound of voices speaking in hushed tones.

Even though she could barely hear them through the door of her bedroom, something about the cadence of the voices and their hurried, whispered intensity made her sit up, curious to know what had disturbed the tranquil normalcy of the morning household. Sliding her legs from beneath the covers, she stood and went to the door where she listened carefully for the sound of footsteps in the upstairs.

Her body felt light, less heavy, her mind clearer, just as it had every day so far, as if she were emerging from a long convalescence. She could not remember when anyone had ever forbidden her to do anything she wished in this house, her intuition told her that whatever was being whispered about downstairs concerned her but was something she was not supposed to hear.

Hearing no sounds nearby, Sarah opened her bedroom door, glanced up and down the hallway, and, finding it clear, she tiptoed across to the bedroom directly opposite hers. There she crossed to the window that looked down on the driveway on the front side of the house, seeing two black, chauffeur-driven Rolls Royce's in the gravel circle, their engines idling and their drivers behind the wheels.

Her reporter's curiosity prickling to know the identities of the people downstairs, Sarah slipped back into the hallway and crept down toward the landing to see if she could pick out the words and glimpse the faces of the visitors. At first all she could hear was a continuation of the intense whispering, but she picked up enough inflection to understand that two of the whisperers were men, and she heard a third set of whispers that she knew belonged to Jessica Lodge. Whatever the discussion was about, too few of the words made it up the stairs for Sarah to know any more than that they were talking about a process and the need to hurry it along and that something else was happening that was adding to the risk of this process. Finally, Jessica Lodge seemed to have heard enough because her voice suddenly rose from a whisper to a tone loud enough for Sarah to hear very clearly as the words came out imperious and final. "I understand your feelings, but the answer is absolutely not. I cannot allow anything to disrupt our plans when I am so close!"

Next came an angry rumbling from the other voices, but Jessica seemed to hold fast. A moment later, Sarah heard the front door open again and then close, and assuming the people were leaving, she hurried back to the front bedroom and watched two of the men she had met at dinner in the basement dining room walk back to their respective cars. A second later she tiptoed into her own bedroom and slipped into bed again, pretending to be asleep until Jessica Lodge walked in moments later.

"Still asleep?" Jessica said.

Sarah opened her eyes as if she were just waking up. "Did I oversleep?" she asked in a husky voice.

"No," Jessica said in a light voice, but when Sarah rolled over and looked at her, she could see the red blush in the older woman's cheeks that hinted at anger "Come down and join me for breakfast, and then we can take our walk."

Without appearing to, Sarah studied Jessica and tried to figure out what was different about her. Whatever it was, it wasn't anger, she decided, at least not anger alone. She sensed intensity, focus, a heightened energy, and determination that belied the idea they were just going to enjoy a simple country breakfast and then take a walk. There was a goal here, a purpose, and it had lain below the surface of things the whole time, but it was important.

As soon as Jessica left, Sarah hurried to get ready and then joined the older woman downstairs in the breakfast room about fifteen minutes later. For the first time in—how long had it been? —her reporter's instincts were fir-ng on all cylinders. Jessica poured tea and passed the toast cart and the butter to Sarah. The house cleaner brought in scrambled eggs, sausage, and bowl of fresh fruit. If Sarah hadn't been seeing Jessica so frequently, nothing would have appeared amiss, but because she had, she noted the sharper gleam in Jessica's eyes, saw the slightly quicker movements, detected the slight edge to her voice.

That was why, when it happened, her senses were on full alert. She could not describe the sensation, only that within seven or eight minutes of the time she had sat down at the table something *invisible*, like a shock wave or an energy pulse, rolled through the room. For Sarah it was perceptible, but for Jessica it was profound.

The older woman was raising her teacup to her lips when the wave hit. Jessica froze, eyes widening in shock and her skin going pale in a flash. Her teacup fell from her frozen hand, clattered onto her saucer, and shattered, spilling tea all over the table. Jessica let out a faint cry, then closed her eyes as if she were in great pain, and for a second Sarah was sure the old woman was having a heart attack.

A moment later, as if an earthquake had tremored then passed, the house seemed to return to normal. Sarah reached across the table and took Jessica by the wrist where her fingers were gripping the tablecloth like talons. "Jessica," she said, the words tumbling out, "are you okay? Do you need a doctor?"

Jessica opened her eyes and blinked, her gaze appearing suddenly rheumy and unfocused. She ignored Sarah's question and turned her head in the direction from which the wave had come, which Sarah knew from watching the sun rise and set each day was toward the east.

Sarah watched Jessica closely, seeing her throat contract as she swallowed. Jessica's head remained frozen, staring unseeing into the east until the house cleaner came bustling into the room with a towel and began to mop up the spilled tea, which had run off the table and was dripping into Jessica's lap.

The maid's frantic dabbing snapped Jessica into alertness once again, and she gave her head a little shake. "Are you okay?" Sarah asked again. "Should we call some- one?"

Jessica finally managed to turn toward her. Her eyes slowly came into focus. "No," she said, quite sharply. She looked down at where Sarah's hand grasped her wrist and for the first time seemed to notice she was gripping the bunched tablecloth like a lifeline. With what looked like a grimace of will, she made herself let it go.

"What was that?" Sarah asked. "Was it an earthquake?" "You felt it?"

"Yes," Sarah said, knowing even as she spoke it couldn't have been an earthquake because nothing in the house had shaken. Just behind Jessica's chair stood an antique open cupboard with fragile plates on small wooden stands. Not one of them had so much as tottered.

"It was..." Jessica seemed to search for the right word. "A shift in power."

"What?"

Jessica shook her head. "I can't really explain it."

Sarah looked at the old woman carefully, wondering if what had just happened was connected to the visit by the two men that morning. She realized at the same instant that Jessica Lodge knew damn well exactly what had just happened, but that she wasn't going to offer another word of explanation.

CHAPTER THIRTY-FIVE

C zarnecki waited until they were on the other side of Oswiecim before he took out his cell phone and placed a call to Lisa Giles. He gave a quick report on what had occurred at the scene of the old Auschwitz concentration camp, describing what he had witnessed happening to John and what he had experienced himself when he had touched John and heard the almost indescribable wailing sound that had slowly fallen to silence.

Afterwards he gave a series of yes and no answers, seeming to respond to the questions Lisa Giles asked, and then he handed the phone to John.

As John took the phone, he felt a flurry of anger well up. "What the hell is going on?" he demanded. "Why didn't you or Rabbi Czarnecki tell me what was going to happen?"

"I apologize. We didn't tell you because we weren't sure that anything was going to happen. Please believe me when I say there is so much, we don't know. In any event, what happened to you this morning was extraordinarily important."

"Why is that?"

"Because if I understand properly, you were invested by an incalculable number of spirits."

John said nothing, just closed his eyes and shuddered as the almost unbearable intensity of the combined emotions rolled through him again.

"It also confirmed a theory we had," Lisa Giles went on. "I sent you an email that will explain what I mean."

John shook his head, still feeling as if he had cobwebs in his brain and trying to understand what she was talking about. "What theory?"

"I have no time to explain. If you have questions after you see the email, call me. In the meantime, you need to go to your hotel, collect your bags, and get to the airport. The sooner you are out of Poland, the better it will be for all concerned."

John felt something cold in the pit of his stomach. "Why is that?"

"Because what happened to you at Auschwitz is now known to everyone in the Coven."

"How?"

"They are attuned."

"Well . . . where are we supposed to go?"

"I have already made reservations for you on a flight departing this afternoon."

John rubbed his eyes. "Where to?" "Cambodia."

"Why?" he asked, but even as the words escaped his lips, he was sure he already knew the answer. He felt dread like a block of ice in his stomach.

The next twenty-four hours passed in a sort of blur as they flew from Kraków to Frankfurt, then on to Shanghai and from there, after a seven-hour layover, to Phnom Penh. John spoke little the entire time, feeling as if he was withdrawing deeper and deeper into himself. Part of it was anger and resentment, a lingering feeling that people he knew truly little about were using him because, as Rebecca Nurse had told him back in Salem, *you are the weapon.*

Amy understood his need for silence. She sat beside him for all the interminable hours on the airplanes and in the terminal at Shanghai, respecting the silence that had grown up between them. The only time she tried to shake him out of his torpor was in Shanghai when she downloaded the email from Lisa Giles.

"I think you need to see this," she said, handing him her laptop.

He took it without comment.

The first part of the email was a reproduction of the piece of paper John had photographed in the Rare Book Collection at the Phillips Library, showing the unknown house with the lines extending from the gables. The second sheet was a drawing of the House of the Seven Gables, showing its orientation to the four points of the compass and then extending the same kind of lines from its gables. The third sheet was a map of the world with the lines drawn from both houses crossing in a number of places.

The first place that caught his eye was a point in northern Europe. "That's where we just were, isn't it?" he asked pointing his finger to where the ley lines crossed at a point just east of Oswiecim, Poland.

Amy nodded. "Yes."

He looked closer at the map and what he saw next made the breath catch in his throat. Their next destination was right outside Phnom Penh, and that was exactly where another set of the lines crossed. He saw more lines that crossed in Rwanda, Africa, and he thought of the Hutus and Tutsis and the war between the two where hundreds of thousands died. More lines crossed at Moscow, and he thought of Stalin's purges.

"What do these lines mean?" he asked, hearing the slight tremor in his voice.

"I think they mark places in the world where great evil can take place, or where evil has taken place, or where the Devil's influence is strongest."

"But the evil hadn't taken place in most of these places before that first map was drawn."

"I know."

"So, the House of the Seven Gables, was that built to mark out the evil places, or to somehow help them become what they became?"

"Are you asking if the houses themselves are more intimately connected with the Devil?"

John nodded. "What if they are more than just old houses? What if they are more powerful than we ever would have guessed and those houses and the way those lines cross create places where terrible evil is more possible than in other places?"

He looked at her as she studied the papers and wondered if she had known this all along, in conjunction with other things she had known and not shared with him, like her knowledge of Lisa Giles, like her coming to the *Salem News* from the FBI with the goal of protecting him. Thinking about the misdirection and secrecy and manipulation made him angry.

He knew he was the weapon, and that his allies were bleeding information out to him at a pace that assured they'd keep control. He wanted to get his daughter back, but they all wanted something much bigger, namely the defeat of the Coven. John wanted to defeat the Coven, too, but not as his first step. First, he wanted Sarah back. He suspected his "allies" didn't want that because it meant they might lose control. The problem was he now knew Amy had been working with Lisa Giles and other members of the anti- Coven force for a while, and if push came to shove, he wasn't certain whether her loyalty lay primarily with them or with him. How was he ever going to know for sure what she would do or to whom she would be loyal?

CHAPTER THIRTY-SIX

B y the time they came off the plane into the heat and humidity of Cambodia, John was exhausted, partly by the stress of the trip and his inability to sleep for more than short bursts, but more because of his continuing recollection of what had happened to him at Auschwitz and what he feared was going to be repeated somewhere outside the city of Phnom Penh. Still, he knew that his life might depend on his being as alert as possible, and he struggled with only limited success against the lethargy that seemed to have seeped into his very bones.

He and Amy stood in the customs line watching their fellow passengers as they had done in each of the airports they had flown through, looking for anyone who was paying too much attention or any sign they were being followed. Echoing Lisa Giles, Czarnecki had told them before they left Kraków that the Coven could not have failed to register what had happened when they went to Auschwitz and therefore, they needed to exercise great care on the remain- der of their journey. John wondered if he would ever again be able to look at other people normally and not question whether all of them—the businessperson, the tourist, the flight attendant, the mother pushing a stroller, the police-man—were members of the Coven.

Seeing no one who was paying them too much attention, they reached the head of the customs line, went through, and had their passports stamped and then went to claim their luggage. Outside the luggage claim they spotted the man they had been told to look for. There was little doubt he was the right one because Lisa had texted them a picture of a one-armed man in the orange robes of a Buddhist monk. In the picture the man's face was round as a Buddha's. The chin cleft, a thick scar from above the left eyebrow down across the left cheek all the way to the man's chin bisected it. John doubted that not even the Coven could have found a man with the same face and the same missing left arm.

As they walked up to him, the man brought one hand to his forehead and bowed his head slightly in a one-handed version of the usual Buddhist greeting. Amy also made a *wai* bow, bringing both hands to her forehead. "Master Viphop?" John asked, as he copied Amy's bow.

"Yes," the man said quietly, shooting a quick look around.

"Welcome to Cambodia. We go."

"If you don't mind, I have to use the restroom first," John said.

Master Viphop make a small grimace but pointed to a sign on the wall. "We wait here for you."

John left his bags and walked quickly to the restroom but paused at the door to make sure it appeared safe. Going over to the urinal, he unzipped and stood with his eyes unfocused, feeling the weight of his exhaustion settle on his shoulders.

He gave a cursory glance over his shoulder as two men who looked Cambodian walked in, and then he turned back toward the wall. He was starting to turn away from the urinal when he noticed one of the Cambodian men was standing behind him while the other one had remained by the door with his foot against it to keep anyone else from coming in.

He glanced down at the closest man's hand, saw the knife, and realized in an instant it was too late to do anything because it was already moving toward him and there was absolutely no way to stop it. He opened his mouth, instinctively preparing to cry out but no sound came forth. Instead, something inside him, something alien he hadn't even suspected was there, but which had been waiting, coiled like a deadly snake, reacted with explosive joy.

John had no time to understand when, rather than a pan- icked cry, a bolt of blinding light shot from his gaping mouth and hit attacker high in the chest. There was no sound, but the damage was the same as twelve-gauge shotgun would make if fired at pointblank range with a load of buckshot. The man flew backwards, his knife clattering uselessly onto the tiles, his upper chest and his throat now a gaping hole.

The thing inside John wasn't done. He felt its wave of elation and its thirst for vengeance and knew he was powerless to stop it. The second man who had stayed by the restroom door gaped at John, his eyes wide open and white with panic, but he was trying to get something out of his pocket. Knowing even before got it free that it had to be a gun, John pointed his right hand at the man. John understood he could not risk opening his mouth or pointing the palm of his hand as he had done in the catacombs beneath Salem, both of which would produce a shotgun like blast, he pointed three fingers at the man's chest. Three separate bolts, each one like firing a pistol rather than a shotgun blast, shot out of the ends of his fingers and hit the man, one in the stomach and two in the upper chest. His hand stopped reaching for his gun as he fell to the ground. Shocked with himself and horrified by what he'd done, just as he'd been in the catacombs beneath Salem, John also felt the overwhelming elation that came from striking back at the Coven. That part of him hungered for more Coven members to come pouring through the door; it hungered to kill and kill and kill until there were no more Coven members alive.

John swallowed hard, recognizing that he needed to control whatever this thing was inside him, calm himself down, and get out of the bathroom as quickly as possible without calling any more attention to himself. Grabbing a paper towel from the dispenser on the wall by the sinks, he wiped off the flush handle of the urinal and then hurried out the door, step- ping past the dead man and using the paper towel to grasp the handle.

When he got back into the terminal, he kept his head turned toward the ground and hurried across to where Amy waited with Master Viphop. "Let's go," he said in a low tone.

"Trouble?" Master Viphop asked. "Yes."

"Come quick," the monk said as he turned and hurried through the crowd.

CHAPTER THIRTY-SEVEN

T hey walked out of the airport terminal and stood in front of a line of taxis where Master Viphop negotiated with one of the drivers about where they wanted to go. Master Viphop and the driver finally settled on a price, and the monk signaled for Amy and John to climb into the back of the Toyota minivan. John glanced nervously over his shoulder as they climbed into the taxi, but there still did not seem to be a commotion inside the terminal that would indicate that the bodies had been discovered.

As they drove away from the terminal, John looked over his shoulder, trying to pick out anyone who might have run out from the terminal and jumped into a taxi behind them or a car that suddenly pulled away from the curb and started to follow. He saw nothing unusual.

The taxi drove out of the airport and into the confusion of Cambodian traffic. They moved slowly, the driver speeding up then slamming on the brakes, honking, and swerving around bicycles laden with supplies, overburdened trucks, animals, and other cars. John felt the humid air like another layer of clothing and breathed in the unfamiliar scents. He looked out the window but barely registered the scenery, his mind too taken up with trying to figure out if they were being followed and at the same time replaying the scene in the bathroom over and over. He glanced down at his hands and felt a growing dread at what he was now certain was about to happen.

Father Faust had called it "being invested" and had emphasized how extraordinary it was that John could be invested by more than one spirit at a time. Of course, Faust had also despised him for that same ability, wanting to use him to help destroy the Coven but then making certain John's ability died along with John in the final struggle.

John shuddered as he thought about what was about to happen to him, and for half a second he thought he could understand Faust's point of view. Being invested wasn't *natural*, and it wasn't *right*. It was more like being invaded, having things jammed inside that had no weight or substance but which took up room, nonetheless. Spirits that carried the terror, anger, pain, and sorrow that still lingered from their horrible deaths. Otherwise, how could he have reacted fast enough to stop a man who had already started to thrust a knife at his belly?

The fact he had survived the attack made him grateful, yet the fact he'd had no control over his reaction terrified him. What else were these spirits liable to do? Just because they had saved him didn't mean he could trust their actions in the future, did it? He was their host, and they needed to keep him alive. But then again, if these spirits that had invaded him could give him the power to get Sarah back safely, then whatever the cost it had to be bearable.

His thoughts were interrupted when the taxi driver slowed down and pulled off the road. Master Viphop nodded. "We get out here," he said.

They came to a stop and climbed out of the taxi in a dusty, unpaved parking area. Ahead of them in English, Cambodian, and other languages, a sign pointed toward a building in the distance and read "Choeung Ek Village," and below it in smaller letters something about the Killing Fields. John could see the tour busses parked ahead of them and lines of tourists walking toward a tall, graceful structure in the distance. Small clusters of Buddhist monks stood around the corners of the parking area, and guards or policemen in official-looking uniforms patrolled.

Master Viphop paid the driver, and as the taxi drove away John could see the monk turn slowly and look around with care. As he did, he noticed that Viphop's eyes stopped as he made eye contact with the monks. Each time he did, the other monk gave a nod, which John hoped meant an all clear, that there was no sign of the Coven. So far, John had said nothing to either Amy or Viphop about the attack in the men's room. In Viphop's case, the monk was a stranger, and he didn't yet trust him enough to admit he had just killed two men back at the air- port. Where Amy was concerned, she had kept so much from him, he didn't want to share the information even though he knew he should.

Master Viphop pointed toward the tall structure in the distance, and they began walking down a path that led through a green area with random indentations in the earth. As soon as they walked between the first of the indentations, John heard it, the wailing and clamoring from millions of tortured throats, the fingernails-on-a-blackboard sound that made him want to turn and run away.

Somehow, he resisted the urge to flee and kept himself walking forward. *Why am I doing this?* he wondered, even as he put one foot in front of the other. In the next second he began to feel it, the sense of strangers inhabiting him, crawling into his head, into his psyche, first hundreds and then thousands and then hundreds of thousands, all of them sharing his identity and his being like they were bunkmates sharing a room.

His sanity broke loose, flapping like a loose shingle during a hurricane. Still, he put his leg forward. He took a step, then another. *Why am I doing this?* he asked, the question rolling silently through his mind as he suffered the violation of spirits beyond number invading his being.

Even as he asked the question he knew the answer, because along with the assault he had another sense, that the spirits were like the passengers on a sinking ocean liner, and he was the lifeboat. For reasons he could not explain, and he could only guess, he offered them a chance for peace, and yes, for vengeance. Whatever gift or ability or curse had brought him to this place, he knew in his gut he was the *only* alternative to the screaming and wailing and reliving of their final terrible moments that these spirits possessed.

He was the weapon, and now he was the lifeboat, too. Having passed the point of speech or conscious thought,

he was barely aware of Amy holding one arm and Viphop holding the other as he put one foot in front of the other and took another step. Even so, terribly aware of his own sensations—the fear, the unutterable pain, the sense of violation and loss of control—he thought again he was losing the last fragile grasp on his sanity.

He could not have said how long it took to reach the tall pagoda-like memorial structure, but he knew the tourists he had seen earlier had somehow cleared away and all the Buddhist monks who had been in the parking area had materialized around him. Viphop pulled open the doors of the structure, and whatever pain John had experienced earlier doubled as the wailing and the feeling of assault intensified.

John felt his knees buckle and arms come around him to hold him up as, barely able to move now, he inched his way toward the rack of skulls. His conscious thoughts were

all about self-preservation. They told him to turn and get away, but his body kept moving forward as if under the control of another person. Signs he could barely see through the tears that streamed from his eyes warned people in various languages not to touch the skulls. As deep as he was in the throes of his agony, John saw one other thing.

A face appeared before him, and although everything else was a terrible blur he could see it clearly and he felt a sudden calm. Rebecca Nurse stood looking at him and smiling. It was an enigmatic smile that held warmth, compassion, regret, and need, all at the same time, and he knew without any need for words what it was she needed. Not knowing if he could stand any more but knowing while he could not refuse, he stopped fighting the pain and the violation and the loss of self and thrust his hands toward the skulls. As he did, a feeling more jolting than electricity and hotter than lava shot through his flesh, but he did not stop.

The moment he touched the skulls he wondered if he had finally lost consciousness because the noise ceased and along with it the sensation that his nerves were in a molten conflagration. Somewhere inside himself he had the feeling as if all the people who had ever massed in Tiananmen Square at one time had suddenly fallen silent. A feeling of peace stole over him, and he sagged against the arms that held him and heard himself whimper in the sudden silence. He felt hands wiping his face and saw a bloody towel as an orange arm dabbed the blood that poured from his nose.

He didn't know how long it took for him to be able to stand on his own, five minutes, fifteen. For that entire time, he had the sense that a large group of orange-robed monks were gathered around him, forming a protective barrier, and keeping all other people away from the memorial building. When he was finally able to stand on his own and when the mucous and blood had stopped flowing from his nose and ears, he stood blinking in the sunlight that streamed through the open doors.

The monks turned toward him, and as a group they put their joined hands to their foreheads and bowed in a long, formal acknowledgement of what he had just endured. John looked at them, unable to fully understand what had just happened, but knowing that beyond his powers to describe it, he was a changed man. He knew this and accepted it. He felt less than he had been before because he had given up part of himself, but he was also more than he had ever imagined being.

And now it was time to get Sarah.

PART III

CHAPTER THIRTY-EIGHT

Two days after the incident at the breakfast table when Sarah had been afraid Jessica was having a heart attack, they were out together on their daily walk, meandering toward the top of one of the endless pastures on Jessica's estate. When they reached the top, Jessica stopped and pointed eastward.

"This is the highest point on the property. You can see the English Channel," she said.

In the distance, two miles or so, Sarah thought, she could see the white-capped, slate blue waters of the North Atlantic. The sight made her think of Boston and her job and her father, and for the first time since she had been there, she felt a twinge of homesickness and a readiness to return to her world.

When she turned away from the view, she found Jessica studying her. "Are you thinking about home?" "How did you guess?"

"Something in your expression I haven't seen before."

Sarah nodded. "I was just wondering when it was going to be time to go back."

"Soon, my dear. There's just one more thing we need to do together and then I think everything will be prepared."

"What will it be?"

Jessica took her arm and started to walk her down the other side of the pasture. Just as had happened the last time Jessica touched her like that, Sarah felt a burst of happiness and protection, as if this woman wanted only what was best for her, and along with it she felt a surge of trust.

"All in good time," Jessica said. "I want it to be a surprise."

They walked down the hill, past a flock of sheep that hurried away from them as they began to come close. Gulls wheeled in the air overhead and cried out. The sky was gray, an endless plain of clouds stretching as far at the eye could see.

They had reached the halfway point in the pasture, and Sarah could see a dirt road below them with a stone wall running beside it. A huge tree stood below and to the left, and there the dirt road seemed to disappear into a dark copse of trees. Beside the huge tree a deserted-looking stone barn with broken windows and missing roof shingles helped darken the scene, throwing everything around it in deep shadow.

Continuing down, they had almost reached the road when it hit, a wave of force that didn't seem to disturb the sheep or the gulls or even tremble a blade of grass, but which felt to Sarah like it was more powerful than the one they had felt at breakfast two days earlier. It staggered her as if she had tripped, but she managed to stay on her feet. Jessica uttered a cry, and when Sarah turned to look at her, she saw the older woman grab her chest and fall to her knees.

"Jessica!" she cried, rushing over, and dropping to the ground beside her.

Jessica's eyes were bouncing around, her gaze seeming unhinged. "Are you okay?" Sarah asked.

"I... I don't know." "What was that?"

"A change in one of the vortices," Jessica said, her voice a weak rasp. "That's the only thing it could be."

"I don't understand," Sarah said, feeling a sudden tingle of fear.

"It means we failed to stop something from happening." Jessica's eyes came into focus, and she saw Sarah's face. "It means you will be leaving sooner than I might have wished, my dear."

Jessica put her hands behind her and tried to push herself up. "Help me get up," she said to Sarah, her voice strengthening. "I have things I need to do."

Sarah stood and leaned down to help Jessica. Her heart was pounding because in the last few seconds a curtain seemed to have dropped away. She suddenly realized more

than any other time since she had arrived here that things far more complex than she had previously suspected were going on all around her and that she was a pawn in someone's complicated plan.

"Quickly, my dear," Jessica said, standing as Sarah helped her up and seeming to recover completely and with amazing speed. "Time is very short."

CHAPTER THIRTY-NINE

The monks formed a cordon around John and Amy and moved them back to the parking lot where Master Viphop flagged a second taxi.

"Where are we going?" Amy asked.

"Airport," Master Viphop said as he climbed into the taxi without the customary bartering and ordered the man to drive them to the airport.

"We don't have a reservation," Amy said. "No matter."

"What do you mean?" Amy asked.

Mast Viphop cast his eyes toward the driver in the front seat and shook his head. Minutes later, after speeding up and slamming on the brakes and swerving around bikes, busses, and trucks, they pulled into the airport where the driver demanded what Master Viphop thought was an excessive sum but paid it anyway.

They climbed out of the taxi and Master Viphop waited for the driver to pull away before he took them to a second taxi and told them to get inside. Master Viphop gave the man directions and they pulled away from the terminal, but instead of leaving the airport, they wound around the interior roads and ended up at a smaller building with private jets parked on the other side.

"You go here," the monk said, and he handed them a slip of paper with an airplane's tail number written down.

"Where are they taking us?" Amy demanded, her voice taking on a hint of alarm.

Again, Master Viphop glanced at the driver and shook his head. "Go," he said. "Hurry."

"But who's paying?" Amy said, still not moving. "We don't have this kind of money!"

"Not worry," Viphop said. "Many, many people pay, and we pray for good thing." He nodded toward John.

John had been sitting quietly and not saying a word. He felt like a man swimming in a huge ocean on the darkest night of the year, but now he turned toward the monk and nodded. "Thank you," he said.

John and Amy went into the small private terminal, showed piece of paper with the tail number to the woman behind the reception desk, who pointed to one of the planes, a small Lear parked at the end of the row. They went outside the rear door and onto the tarmac, where they could see two pilots doing a walk-around check of the aircraft.

As John walked up, one of the pilots turned and gave a welcoming nod. "If you're ready to go, sir, we can be wheels up in ten minutes."

John was surprised to see what he thought was a British Army uniform. He held out his hand. "You are?"

"Major Howard Prentice, sir."

John looked at him in momentary confusion. "Are you here on official business?"

"No, sir. I happen to be a chaplain in Her Majesty's Army, but I'm also licensed to fly jets. I'm on leave. This flight has nothing to do with the British military. It's against regulations to wear the uniform when I'm on my own time, but in this case, I thought it might provide a little insurance in case we needed help defusing a tricky situation."

"Like what?"

"I think you'd know that better than I would, sir. Best if we get you and the lady on board so we don't have that risk." John nodded and went up the steps on to the small jet, and Amy came after. Master Viphop came as far as the top

step where he bowed again.

"I wish you great success against all evil," he said, then disappeared out the door and back down the stairs.

A moment or two later Major Prentice and the co-pilot were both back aboard, the doors were closed, and the jet was moving toward the end of the taxiway to begin its takeoff. As quickly as they turned onto the main runway, the engines cycled up to full throttle and the plane shot forward. They were off the ground, and John sat back in his seat and closed his eyes. He knew he ought to be feeling a huge measure of relief because there was no doubt in his mind the Coven had more people than just the two in the bathroom whose job it was to try and stop him.

He didn't fully understand what had happened to him at Auschwitz and in the Killing Fields outside of Phnom Penh, but he thought that relieving the torment of those spirits must have been a blow to the Coven all by itself. He understood that those spirits provided him with the power he needed to face Jessica Lodge. He just hoped what-ever power he had was going to be enough to defeat Jessica and bring Sarah safely home.

Amy interrupted his thoughts when she reached out and put her hand on his arm. "I know we have a lot to talk about," she said, her voice soft and tentative.

He closed his eyes as the emotions he had been trying and mostly succeeding in keeping buried suddenly welled to the surface. "Yes," he said.

"I know you're very disturbed that I held things back, but I hope you can understand I thought I had good reasons.

"When were you planning on telling me the truth?" he demanded, finally turning to look at her.

"I wanted to so many times, but I couldn't seem to pick the right moment."

"What about after we made love? Was that about us or was it a Wiccan ritual?"

Amy closed her eyes and a tear tickled out of the corner of one eye. "I would never have slept with you for any reason other than wanting to be with you. That came from my heart. Do you believe that?"

John shook his head. "I wish I did. I don't know who any-body is anymore or why they do what they do. I don't trust anybody I see because I wonder if every one of them works for the Coven. I don't know whether you really worked for the FBI, or who Lisa Giles takes her orders from. I don't know who sent this jet to pick us up or who ordered Master Viphop or Rabbi Czarnecki to meet us and take us places.

"Who's pulling the strings? I know somebody is. Are they good guys or bad guys? I don't even know who I am anymore because of the things that have happened to me. I just know I need to get my daughter back, and when that's done, I need to sort my life out, starting with getting honest answers."

"What happened to you back at the Killing Fields?" "You know what happened," John snapped. "I was

invaded by spirits. I don't know how many—hundreds of thousands, millions—and they screamed and cried, and I couldn't stand it."

"And what stopped the screaming?"

John looked at her, feeling his anger and resentment and self-pity all bubbling up and mixing together, and knowing them for exactly what they were, but feeling that he richly deserved to feel that way. "She was there, and she forced me to touch the skulls."

"Rebecca?" John nodded.

"She forced you?"

John pressed his lips together in anger, but finally he said. "She made me trust that it was the right thing to do."

Amy nodded. "I thought it was her. I felt something there." "I'm tired of trusting, Amy. I've spent my life digging up

the facts, and I need to find the facts here."

"What if there are no facts? What if there are just a bunch of beliefs in an un-provable God or gods or Superior Being, and what if those beliefs are all different except in one thing, and that is that they believe in the sanctity of life and in the positive direction of the universe? In other words, they believe in creation and the possibility of love and compassion, as opposed to destruction and hatred. What if that's all you can get?"

"There still must be people in charge. There's money for a jet, so there has to be some kind of organization."

"What if it's just a few anonymous donors and a loose, informal gathering of like-minded people?"

John shook his head. "I don't believe it. I've never seen anything like that in my life."

"Maybe there's a first time for everything."

John shrugged. She was right, but part of him cried out for an answer. The bottom line where he was dealing with facts as opposed to supposition and belief. He felt a terrible blast of loneliness, but in the absence of something he could prove to himself, a hard base on which he could sustain a belief in the rational aspects of everything he was doing, he preferred solitude. "That's not good enough," he said.

He closed his eyes, reclined his seat, and slept for at least three hours until the co-pilot touched his arm to wake him. "Excuse me, sir, but we'll be setting down in Abu Dhabi for refueling. Be on the ground about thirty minutes and then off again. Going to ask you to sit up and prepare for landing."

John sat up, rubbed his eyes, and looked out the window at the sand-scorched Mideast flatness extending in all directions.

"I'll be getting off here, and there will be a new co-pilot for the last leg into London," the co-pilot said. "We'll be bringing food on board. Sandwiches and wraps, or do you have any special requests?"

John shook his head. "I'll eat whatever you've got," he said, and felt the plane begin to lose altitude as it began its approach toward Abu Dhabi.

The jet came in for a gentle landing, and they waited in the baking heat for the fuel trucks to top off their tanks. The co-pilot got off, and a bearded man got on, bringing a cooler packed with sandwiches, as well as hummus, baba ghanoush, and fresh fruit.

John looked out the window as the plane began to taxi again, his thoughts turning bitter and ever inward. It seemed to him that the parched desert landscape of Abu Dhabi mirrored what he felt inside, his sense of emotional aridity, a feeling as if his connections with other people and even with himself had been scorched away. He felt isolated and untouchable in one sense, and in another as if his sense of self, his individuality had been completely subsumed by the spirits or souls that flowed into him almost like an unstoppable river churning into his mouth and down his throat, the volume impossible to contain and beyond measure yet still pouring into him and into him alone and yet somehow being contained.

As they reached the end of the runway and moved into position for takeoff, Amy touched his arm. "John?" she said. He turned to look at her, and whatever she saw in his eyes seemed to be all the answer she needed. She pulled her hand away quickly and turned to look out the opposite window. John looked at her for another second and thought he could see the shiny track of a tear as it slid from her eye and ran down her cheek.

CHAPTER FORTY

John slept for another three or four hours and woke up again when the new co-pilot tapped him on the arm. "Food, sir?" the man asked, holding out a couple of sandwiches.

John stretched. "How much more time to London?" "About two hours."

John took one of the sandwiches that was labeled chicken salad. "Thank you," he said as he tore off the wrapping and took a big bite. He took a bag of chips from a proffered basket and a Diet Coke. As soon as he started eating, he realized how hungry he had been and quickly wolfed down the sandwich and the bag of chips.

Amy was sleeping, so he stood up to stretch his legs, went to the bathroom, and on his way back decided to go

up to the cockpit. As he started walking in that direction, he felt a sudden lethargy, and his body seemed very heavy. He wondered if he'd been sitting on the plane so long that he'd developed a blood clot. It seemed hard to think suddenly, but his brain told him that a blood clot would not make him sleepy.

He went to the cockpit door and pushed it open, needing to tell the pilot that he was feeling strangely ill. When he looked at the back of the pilot's head, at first it made no sense. He saw the small hole in the man's skull and the trickle of blood that ran down to his collar and that had spread along his shoulder and dripped on to floor.

He blinked hard thinking his brain wasn't working right because he couldn't be seeing this. He looked over at the co-pilot who had turned to glance over his shoulder. "Wha—" John said. He was trying to get the question out of his mouth, but his lips and tongue felt like it was covered with glue. "What issss?" he said again, hearing the words slur.

"Change of plans," the pilot said. "Go sit down before you fall down."

John closed his eyes for just a second, but when he opened them again, he was sitting on the floor looking up at the co- pilot. He shook his head trying to clear it, wanting to tell the man that he had expected the Coven to make its move and that he had known that somehow this was supposed to hap- pen, but before he could even try to form a sentence in his mind everything went dark.

He woke up sometime later in the back of a vehicle. He was parched, and he had a splitting headache as if he were coming off an exceedingly long bender and was horribly hung-over. He felt the road rocking beneath him, heard the bump of tires hitting rough spots in the road. The co-pilot was looking down at him with a placid expression. "Wel- come to England," he said as he brought a hypo- dermic syringe into sight and stabbed it into John's arm.

Darkness returned.

When he woke up a second time he was sitting upright. His head still pounded, his vision blurred, and he had a sense of heaviness in his limbs as if he weighed hundreds of pounds. He was sitting at a table and could make out the shapes of people facing him across the way.

He closed his eyes very slowly and opened them again, hoping to clear his vision, then he moved his tongue around the inside of his mouth trying to generate enough saliva to speak. "Jessica?" he said, in a hoarse voice.

"Yes, John."

He closed his eyes again, tried to gauge the amount of drugs that had to be in his system. A serious tranquilizer. Every motion took all his energy

"I guess you were expecting me," he whispered.

"We have known for some time you would show up here." He nodded, trying without seeming to do so to assess his arms and legs, determine how he was bound, and get a sense of whether he could fight the drugs in his system.

"And Sarah?" he rasped. "Is she here?" "Sarah is sleeping, but she's just fine, John." "And Amy?"

"Amy is also fine."

He nodded, flexing his hands against the thick arm of a wooden chair, doing the same with his leg muscles, unable to move more than his fingers and toes. He was tightly bound to the arms and legs of the chair, and there were bindings around his chest, as well. They were taking no chances.

"Could I have a little water, please?"

Off to his right he heard someone stir. A chair leg scraped against a stone floor and a second later a straw was placed between his chapped lips. He sucked greedily until it was pulled away.

He swallowed, worked his jaw back and forth, tried to make his mind work against the drugs. "I met some of your friends in a men's room in the Phnom Penh airport," he said, his voice coming louder and stronger.

"That was inelegant on our part," Jessica said. "For what it's worth, I was against trying it."

"I seem to have been a terrible inconvenience."

"You have been a challenging opponent, John," Jessica Lodge said. "I have to congratulate you. A year or two ago I thought we were going to be able to check you off our list. After your wife's death, you were on your way to a life of alcoholism, and I hoped you would just slide quietly into ineptitude."

"Sorry to disappoint." He had been blinking his eyes slowly to try and clear them, and this time when he opened them, he found he could make out the shape of the table and the faces. The room was elaborate, with ornate moldings along the ceiling, oil paintings on the walls, but windowless. It brought back terrible memories of the room in the catacombs beneath Salem, and for a moment he could feel the tickle of fear like a small fire starting deep in his belly.

The table was in the form of a hexagram, but instead of being pointed, each arm of the hexagram had a place for a person to sit. John occupied one of those spots, and he could see that each of the other points was also occupied. He looked first to his left and then right, seeing gray hair and erect carriage. They were strangers, but their tailored clothing, rich jewelry, and chiseled features found them as individuals of wealth and power.

John blinked to clear his vision a bit more and finally moved his gaze directly across the table where he knew Jessica Lodge was sitting. He saw her sharing one of the points with a tall man with a full head of gray hair, a ramrod straight nose, strong chin, and regal bearing. Jessica's hair was care- fully done, her gown was long and flowing, and a large sapphire at her throat gave her an almost regal aura.

John looked at her and a tremor of anger replaced the fear he had felt just a moment earlier. Then he moved his eyes to Jessica's left and his breath caught in his throat. Sarah sat along one side of the point, also in a flowing gown, also with her hair up in a formal arrangement, her makeup carefully applied.

"Sarah," he said in a choked voice.

CHAPTER FORTY-ONE

She turned to look at him, but her gaze was blank, lacking recognition, as if she were in a trance or as if she was a stranger who simply looked identical to his daughter.

"Sarah," he said again, hearing the beseeching tremor in his voice. She continued to look at him without any emotion, as implacable as a robot, and he realized she must be drugged or in a trance.

"What do you want?" he asked Jessica.

"John, you've always been so terribly intuitive. You know what we want."

"Well, I presume from the way those two men acted in the airport that you want me dead."

Jessica smiled at him. "See, I told you that you would get it."

"If you want me dead, why even bother with this séance? Why not just kill me?"

He caught the sideways glance Jessica shared with the man who sat beside her.

"We decided to give you one last chance to join us." John snorted a laugh. "Would you believe me if I told you I'd had a change of heart?"

Jessica smiled and shook her head. "Probably not.

John's brain was still stuck in sludge, but his gut instinct told him he needed to play for time. He didn't have a clue how it was going to help him, but he also knew he had no other choice. "So that doesn't really answer my question, does it? What is the point of having me here at this table? Why don't you just shoot me and get it over?"

He saw the people around the table cast glances at each other, as if this idea were a risk to them.

He had already started to suspect that in addition to slowing his mental reactions. He knew they were awfully close to killing him, but he couldn't seem to summon much in the way of either fear or rage.

"Enough," Jessica said. "It is time."

The man who was sitting beside her stood up and walked around the table until he stood directly behind John. At that point Jessica leaned forward and extended her arms to either side. One by one the people around the table reached out and clasped hands. John was relieved to see they bypassed Sarah, but they linked hands with the man standing right behind his chair.

John felt a tremor of fear in his stomach, but nothing more. In a small corner of his brain, he realized he was about to be a passive bystander at his own execution. A second later another realization dawned: it wasn't going to be just him that died. Somehow, by giving them a place to escape into, he had brought freedom to countless spirits that had been held in ongoing torment for an exceedingly long time. If he let himself die, didn't he risk returning these spirits to the agony they had just escaped?

Across the table from where he sat, Jessica Lodge released herself from the chain of hands, stood, and fetched something from a side table behind her. She returned to the table with a bowl and brought it around to each set of joined hands. Dip- ping her hand into the bowl, she proceeded to draw an X on each set of hands with what John knew right away had to be human blood.

When she finished going around the table and each set of hands had a large X that touched each hand equally, she did the same thing to each of her hands and joined them again with the people to either side of her. When that was finished the man who had been standing behind John began to chant.

John paid no attention to the words because right away he became aware that the light in the room seemed to dim, and then a second later he realized it wasn't the light in the room but the light in the immediate circle that had grown darker. As the man behind John continued to chant, the others at the table also began to speak the words with him, and as they did the air within the circle of hands grew even darker.

As the air around him darkened, it also seemed to thicken, and John could feel his chest begin to strain as he tried to pull air into his lungs. His brain was still too muddy to put coherent thoughts together, but he knew he should feel panic. In his mind a faint voice was crying out, telling him he was going to die very soon if he didn't do something. Another part of his brain was trying to put together a question: why was the Coven doing this to him? Why not just cut his wrists and let him bleed to death in yet another of their blood sacrifices? There had to be a reason they were doing it this way, didn't there? He was so sleepy and lethargic, and it was getting so terribly hard to breathe and even harder to summon the determination to fight it. But then in the next second he felt something touch his hand and it seemed as if a light had come on. He opened his eyes and saw Rebecca Nurse holding both of his hands in hers, and on either side of Rebecca, the line of beseeching faces, young, old, man, woman, thou- sands and thousands and millions of them, running into the

distance.

Fight! a voice called out in his head, the tone blaringly loud and insistent. In that same instant, he began to look into the eyes of the other spirits, spirits that had been imprisoned at Auschwitz and in the Killing Fields of Cambodia, and he saw their hope and their fear, and he felt their pain. The face of a little girl looked up at him, and the wrinkled face of a toothless old woman and a young mother holding a baby to her breast, and in that blinding instant he knew their stories as he knew his own. They exploded inside him like a bomb, and with immediate shattering rev- elation he knew the hopes and dreams and aspirations that had been savagely cut short; he knew their loves and their hatreds and their fears, and he knew their fear of his failure was the one thing that united each and every one of them at that moment.

Fight! The word came again like an irresistible wall of will, and he felt Rebecca Nurse's hands squeeze his until what felt like a shot of adrenaline exploded through them and into his veins. As all of this was happening, John was aware that he hadn't moved. He realized that to anyone watching him the change was imperceptible, but his mind was starting to work again.

He focused on the first thing he needed: air. The dark- ness inside the linked hands of the Coven was like a plastic bag over his head. He was suffocating and the darkness all around him was intensifying and hardening, and if he didn't find a way to breathe very quickly, he was going to pass out and die. John felt like he was in a separate universe, and then he realized that he was, that he couldn't breathe because he was being pulled into an eternal prison of cold and darkness and death.

He looked into Rebecca Nurse's eyes and then into the eyes of the nearest of the millions of spirits, and he sensed something there and realized he could draw upon it if he concentrated hard enough. His lungs were on fire, his body rebelling against the lack of oxygen. The darkness continued to harden around him, becoming a shell of impenetrable onyx, and John realized that in another few seconds it would be too late. If he didn't fight back, he was going to die inside a crypt of darkness.

The eyes, he thought, screaming to himself, feeling the beginning of fear and panic and welcome rage as his mind fought the drugs and managed to kick back into high gear. The eyes.

He looked at the little girl, the old woman, the young mother, he looked at the boy beside her and the man beside him and the next three men and then a group of young girls, and in each set of eyes he caught a small glint of energy and hope, a small shred of determination to fight back. In every case it was a dim light, barely perceptible, but it still existed. He opened his eyes wide, and instead of resenting the invasion of the spirits, instead of feeling compromised and overwhelmed, he invited them into him, he asked for their light and for it to combine with his own. His body was starved of oxygen it wanted to shut down, and he felt the darkness so hard and impenetrable now he could barely see the light in the room beyond its boundary. The light was only a foot or two away in any direction, but he was trapped in a bubble of darkness. With the last vestiges of consciousness, he focused his mind on the outer light. While he knew his own life force was vastly insufficient to reach it, he felt it amplified and bolstered now by that small light that each of the million's spirits offered up to him.

His own quickly dimming light, reinforced, and reflected and supercharged by the millions upon millions of tiny lights offered up by the millions upon millions of souls, became like a fist of light that forced back the darkness, which punched through and for a moment made a hole in the shell of death and entrapment.

John felt air rush through the hole, and along with it the light of the room poured in like a blinding sunrise. In that same instant he heard the voices of the Coven grow louder, their chanting increasing in urgency, the words coming faster, full of desperate emotion. For several seconds, the darkness seemed to deepen and gown even harder, and the hole grew smaller.

But the oxygen had come in, and it went straight to John's brain, and he felt his own internal light intensify. As it did, the light he drew from all the other spirits seemed to grow as well, and John felt his rage build inside like something wild and uncontrollable waking from a deep slumber.

The voices might have been louder, the chanting faster, but John was now able to pull the light from deep inside. How much was his own and how much came from all the other spirits and how much was the result of that light being reflected and reinforced by the joining and yearning of all the spirits now bound together inside of him John could not have said.

He only knew that at some point there seemed to be an explosion. He heard no sound, but saw the blinding flash of light that shattered the darkness like a firebomb going off in the deepest night, and when his eyes readjusted, he saw the aftermath of the explosion, the litter of bodies thrown from the table to the corners of the room, their positions so unnatural that he knew without checking for pulses that they were all dead.

CHAPTER FORTY-TWO

At first his heart went into his throat because he thought Sarah had hit by the blast, but then he saw her, sitting in her chair, looking unruffled with not even a hair out of place, looking as if not even a light breeze had disturbed anything near her. She sat just as she had before, as if she hadn't seen or heard anything and not noticing the bodies that uprooted from their chairs and against the walls when the explosion occurred. Even now her expression remained as placid as that of a store mannequin.

Only one other person sat at the table—Jessica Lodge. She was still in her chair, untouched by the blast and she looked different. Her previously elegant hair was askew, and her face had a deep cut along the left cheek where a flap of skin now hung down, but no blood flowed. John could see her molars through the hole.

Her hands stretched out to either side, just as they had been when she'd been holding hands with her fellow Coven members a few seconds earlier. Her right hand held the fingers and partial hand of the person who had been sitting to her right, and her left hand was empty but looked as if the flesh of her fingers fused together in the fiery blast.

As John watched her, Jessica Lodge blinked at him, and as she did the color of her eyes seemed to shift, deepening from blue to black, as the pupils elongated and became something saurian and inhuman. John squinted and the image of Jessica Lodge seemed to flicker, as if he were seeing two distinct figures both occupying the same space. One figure was Jessica, but a more cadaverous version, with her bloodless cut cheek, her molars showing through, her flesh seeming to shrink tighter and tighter to her bones even as he watched; and the other figure taller and more massive yet still gauntly skeletal, a figure of darkness that peered out at him through its slit pupils, that sat hunched as if it had been sleeping in a confined space for a long, long time and was only now beginning to try and stretch its body to its true height, but a figure with hatred and evil radiating off its charred-looking flesh like heat coming off a red-hot stove burner.

John's heart quickened. He felt fear of this creature and terrible revulsion coiling in his guts. Inside himself he heard the moan as the millions upon millions of spirits reacted to this creature that was and was not Jessica Lodge. John's brain kicked into high gear, his thoughts racing as if Rebecca Nurse were whispering to him, her words coming out almost faster than the ear could hear, or the brain could process. What he realized in that moment was that something unspeakably evil was trying to birth its way into the world, something that lived inside of Jessica Lodge or something that looked out *through* Jessica Lodge from a vastly darker and more terrible place—whatever the exact truth was, it was now trying to enter the world of humans. Knowing instinctively what he needed to do, John closed his eyes and opened himself, dropped every shred of ego and identity, every aspect of uniqueness that made him John Andrews, and like a man throwing his arms wide to welcome the world, he called out to the spirits inside him. He found them waiting. Whatever light they had, whatever glimmer of energy, whatever spirit life they had was focused on him, given to him to use as he would.

Feeling the energy begin to fill him, he felt something else that almost eluded description but which he knew was the supercharging effect of fear, of hatred of evil, of a desire for vengeance over the powers of evil.

He brought up his hands, realizing the ropes that held him had burned away. Aiming his palms at Jessica Lodge and at the creature that was trying to take her place, the creature that had almost succeeded, whose blackness seemed to intensify, whose size seemed to grow as it unfolded, whose radiating evil nearly made it impossible for John to focus his energy, he managed to fix his mind and hone the energy of all the millions of converging spirits into a momentary nova aimed at the birthing creature.

He heard a cry of rage and pain and superhuman anger, but in that same instant he was thrust backward out of his seat and felt his head slam against something hard. Then there was nothing but blackness. And in that moment, as darkness seemed to take over everything, he realized he had lost.

CHAPTER FORTY-THREE

"D ad?"

The voice came from faraway like a hand reaching down through impenetrable darkness to offer a way back to the light.

"Dad?"

John's exhaustion called out to him, told him to lie still, that he had done his job and done it well, that he could allow his heart to stop beating now, let his lungs cease their effort of pulling new air. It was telling him to ignore the voice, that he deserved the rest, that he could let other people carry the burdens from now on.

"Dad? Please..."

A small ember sparked, and as if Sarah's voice were a gentle breeze, it began to glow hotter and add its heat to other embers that had nearly gone out. He felt his lungs inflate as cool air rushed in, and he felt his heart contract, at first slowly, but then faster and with more assurance. He managed to open his eyes and saw Sarah looking down at him.

"Thank God," she said, as if to herself, her eyes brimming with tears that ran down her cheeks. "I thought you were dead. You weren't breathing. You hit your head on something and you're bleeding like hell. Is anything broken? Do you have a concussion?"

John opened his mouth, evaluated his jaw to make sure it worked. He could feel the now cooling blood on his collar and his shoulders and realized Sarah had wrapped his head in a piece of cloth she must have torn from one of the dead men's shirts.

"How long was I out?" he managed. Sarah shrugged. "Maybe five minutes." "What about Jessica?"

"She's dead. They're all dead." She blinked and used her wrist to wipe away her tears. "How did you survive? How did I survive? What happened here?" She looked around at the undisturbed table and the horribly mangled bodies that had been thrown against the walls. "What could have caused this? It's so horrible! Was it a bomb? It had to be explosion, but it doesn't make any sense. We have to call the police. My God!"

Sarah was getting more panicked by the second as she tried unsuccessfully to wrap her mind around the unexplainable.

"Sarah," he said, his voice sharp. He waited until she got enough control to look at him, and he saw the fear in her eyes. "Help me stand up."

"No, you shouldn't move."

"Help me up," he said again, and then he started to roll over, showing her that he was going to get up regardless of what she wanted.

She made a face but took his arm and helped him to stand, and he gritted his teeth against the pain that seemed to shoot through every fiber of his body. When he finally got to his feet the room seemed to spin, and he leaned against the wall and waited for the dizziness to subside.

The act of standing seemed to have started his head bleeding, and Sarah reached up and tightened the makeshift bandage that John realized was a white shirtsleeve. He only knew that because he looked at the floor a few feet away and saw the severed arm lying there. It looked like it had been torn off at the shoulder in the first explosion.

Using Sarah and the wall as crutches, John made his way slowly around the room, stepping over and around the bodies of the other Coven members, seeing with satisfaction that they were all dead, until he got to where Jessica Lodge lay, and he heard Sarah's choked intake of breath.

"Oh my God," she whispered.

There was no question that Jessica was dead. There was a massive hole in her chest about the radius of an artillery shell. However, when John looked at her more closely, there was a question as to whether it could really be Jessica Lodge because her body appeared far more damaged than any of the others, her skin shrunken onto her bones giving her an emaciated look of someone who had just escaped from a concentration camp. Also, her eyes were still open, and John could see that even though they were already clouding over, the pupils were still black and vertically elongated like those of a lizard.

Unlike the other dead Coven members, Jessica's hands and arms had not been blown off or mangled beyond recognition, and that was the thing that John found most disturbing. Her hands did not seem to be something that could have been part of a small woman's body. They were black and elongated, the fingernails inhumanly long, ending in coarse, savage points that could only be claws.

As John stared down at her he shuddered, realizing that something far beyond his ability to understand had been about to take place and narrowly averted. Jessica Lodge, whether she had been fully human or something else, had been transforming into a demon. He had no idea what the thing was that she had been about to become, but he had a sense that no matter how much power he'd been able to harness from the spirits that had entered him, it would not have been sufficient to kill the thing with the slit pupils and the claws of a beast.

He sagged back against the table, and then he remembered. "Amy?" he asked Sarah. "Where is she? Is she…" he let his voice trail off, unable to say the word yet knowing that the fate of anyone captured by the Coven was certainly a horrible and painful death.

Sarah was still holding his arm to keep him from falling.

She shook her head. "I don't know." "Did you see her? Try to remember."

Sarah closed her eyes and ran her fingers through her hair. "I don't remember anything from the night somebody grabbed me when I parked my car on Pickering Wharf when I was coming to your house for dinner. Everything after that is like a dream or being on an extended drug trip. I don't remember seeing Amy. I don't really remember *anything*. How long have I been gone?"

John nodded and tried to think back to how many days it had been since Sarah's abduction, realizing it had only been six or seven days, even though it seemed like months. "You weren't here that long," he said. "A little more than a week." He said it absently, his thoughts focused on Amy. He had barely spoken to her in the past thirty-six hours, feeling angry and offended and hurt when he learned how much she had misled him. Now he just wanted to find her alive and in one piece, and he wanted to start the process of erasing the gulf that had grown between them.

"I feel like I've been in a time warp," Sarah said. "I can't remember anything specific, but I have these visions of walking with Jessica and having pleasant talks." She threw her gaze around the room, looking at the dead bodies again, and John felt the shudder that passed through her body. "Jesus H. Christ," she exclaimed, her voice becoming tinged with hysteria. "What are we going to do?" she demanded as a sob escaped her throat.

"We have to try and find Amy," he said again, struggling to keep his thoughts focused but once again felt knots in his stomach. "Then we have to get out of here."

"But don't we have to call the police?"

"This doesn't need the police. The Coven will clean it up or change it before the police could ever get here."

"The Coven? What's the Coven? Who are you talking about?"

"I'll explain later. First help me find Amy."

"You can barely even walk. I need to call an ambulance." "No ambulance. No phone calls. I *have* to walk. I have

no choice."

With Sarah holding one arm and John leaning on the wall for support, they walked out of the dining room and started to make their way down a long hallway that had a number of doors leading to other rooms. There were no windows, but John felt no surprise at that. He knew they had to be under- ground, just as they had been in the Coven's lair in Salem.

As they reached the first doorway, John came to a stop. "Open the door," he said, steeling himself against what he might find.

CHAPTER FORTY-FOUR

Sarah looked at him, and he could see the fear in her eyes. "Can't we just go?" "Open it," he said.

She let go of his arm, took a deep breath as if she feared that something terrible might come flying out at her, turned the handle, and pushed the door inward. Then, when nothing came hurtling out the door at her, she reached inside, felt around for a light, and turned it on. The room was empty, just consisting of shelving on two walls and a sink on the third wall. Buckets lined two of the shelves, and it had sense of normalcy. John recalled the buckets in the prison rooms in the Coven's catacombs beneath Salem and felt a fresh chill.

The door to the next room was different than the earlier door. Strong bolt locks on the top and bottom of the thick door panel told him exactly that for which the room had been used. If he'd had any question about it, he had none when he spotted the small hatch at the bottom of the door that would allow one of the buckets from the storage room next door to be shoved inside to a prisoner.

"Open it," John said when they came even with the door. Sarah threw the bolts back and with the same obvious reluctance, shoved open the heavy door. There seemed to be no light switches inside, but the light that leaked into the room from the hallway lights illuminated the cell well enough for John and Sarah to see that the room was empty, but also the filthy blanket in one corner and the overturned bucket beside the door.

Sarah let out a gasp as she made mental connections. "Are these . . ."

"Yes," John said. "They're cells for keeping prisoners."

Sarah looked down the hallway at two more identical doors that followed the one they were looking into. "Did you know these would be here?" she asked.

John nodded. "They never put you in one?"

"No, I'm sure I would have remembered, but . . . oh my God. Who would they have kept here?"

"The people they sacrificed." "What?"

"I'll explain later. Just keep going."

They continued down the hall, pushing open both cell doors, but finding them as empty as the first, each one holding only an identical filthy blanket and bucket.

Up ahead of them was the last door that opened off to the side and then a final door at the end of the hallway that John guessed had to lead to a staircase that would take them up to the first floor. When he stopped outside that door, Sarah looked at him, but when she saw the determination in his eyes, she turned the knob and pushed it open.

The first thing John saw was the white tile on the floor, and it made his heart freeze. "Turn on a light," he said in a choked voice as he looked through the dimness at what looked like a dark shape against one wall.

Sarah felt around the inside wall near the door and John heard a click. Then he saw what he had been dreading, and when Sarah saw it, she screamed and backed out of the room in horror.

It was Amy, naked, her body chained to the wall and savagely tortured. Blood pooled at her feet. John felt dizzy, and he gripped the wall to try and stay upright as he felt his knees turn to water. It was only when he heard Amy let out a groan that he found the strength to stay on his feet and even take a few steps toward her.

"Amy," he whispered. "Oh, God, what have they done to you?"

Hearing his voice, Amy managed to raise her head. "John," she said, her voice so ephemeral it was barely audible. "I'm... so sorry."

"For what?" he said, his voice breaking as he took in the unimaginable damage, the cuts up and down her legs, on her abdomen, her viscera peeking out in several places.

He forced himself to swallow and tried to shove down the anguish he felt. "Don't talk," he said, looking around for a key to the shackles that held her. "We're going to get you out of here."

"No," Amy said, her voice strengthening slightly. Her eyes locked with his for a second and then her gaze drifted away over his shoulder. She finally brought her eyes back to his. "Love you," she said.

John nodded, his eyes blurring with tears.

Amy mumbled something else he could barely understand, and then her head dropped on her chest. John reached a handout to touch her neck, desperate to find a pulse. There was nothing. He started to crumple, but felt Sarah's arms come around his chest, holding him up.

The next minutes and hours were a blur as they stumbled up the stairs to the first floor, finding the large house now strangely empty of the servants that had always seemed to bustle around in the background. John reacted like a man too numb to think or act as Sarah took him out into the driveway and pushed him in to the passenger seat of a Bentley that still had the keys in the ignition.

She told him to stay there and went back into the house, returning minutes later with her passport and wallet. He looked at her blankly then shook his head, trying to form coherent thoughts. "The passport? How did they get it? How did you know?" he asked.

Sarah started the car and looked in the rearview mirror as she backed up and maneuvered away from the other cars.

She shook her head. "I don't know. I just knew it was there." John moved a numb hand down to his own trouser pocket, and he patted his leg and felt his own passport where he always kept it. They could go home, he thought. But home

to what?

John watched the countryside go past in a blur as they drove out the gates of Jessica Lodge's estate and turned left, away from Lands' End and toward the rest of Great Britain. They came to a roundabout and Sarah headed north and east and kept in that general direction and after a time they saw signs for London and then signs for Heathrow.

Sarah parked the car in long-term parking, helped John out, and then went back and like a career criminal she wiped the wheel and all the surfaces to erase any fingerprints they might have left. She led her father to the bus and from there to the terminal where they bought two tickets on a flight to Boston.

John followed her through security and sat beside her in the waiting area, feeling like a terribly old man, a man who had been used up by a violent and intense experience. His mind was blank, too stunned, and exhausted for rational thought, but underneath the empty white noise of random thoughts he felt an unspeakable pain welling up like a knife in his heart. Amy, he thought, she had kept things from him but only because she was trying to save him. Why couldn't he have understood and accepted that and at least let their last few days and hours together be something he could look back on with anything but bitter regret?

He turned his head because he felt Sarah's gaze. "Are you okay?" she asked.

"I don't know," he told her. "I'm so sorry about Amy." He nodded. "Thank you."

"What was it she said to you at the very end?"

He closed his eyes and tried to recall those last words she had spoken, words so soft he had hardly been able to make them out. Words that even now left him wondering if he had heard correctly. Amy had looked past him, toward Sarah just before she said it.

"I think she said, 'I'm sorry because I was too late.'" "I wonder what she meant by that?"

He looked at her, his daughter, the one surviving person in his life after the Coven had murdered both women he had loved, and he tried to shove down the fear that nibbled at the corners of his exhausted mind. Things would get better, he told himself. Things would get better because they had to, didn't they?

"I don't know what she meant, not exactly," he told Sarah.

And he hoped it was true.